GIFTS FROM A STALKER

A Rolling Brook Novel

Blye Donovan

ISBN: 9798481252377
Imprint: Independently published
Cover Design by Central Covers.
Series Logo Design by K.B. Barrett Designs.

DEDICATION

To the brave men and women who risk their lives daily in the line of duty. Thank you.

CONTENT WARNING

Contains profanity, mild violence, and mature sexual content. Also introduces survivor's guilt and mentions PTSD and the loss of a parent.

PROLOGUE

Dillon

Dillon walked down the dirt lane toward his brother's house. It was night, and the only illumination came from the stars. The air held a chill, making the hairs on the back of his neck stand up as he reached the turn-off onto Jake's driveway.

His sleeping brain didn't question why he was on foot instead of driving. When his brother's modern ranch home appeared in the distance, Dillon's legs grew heavy, a sense of dread creeping upon him.

The sound of gunshots spun him around, and he searched the darkness for their source. When the shots continued, Dillon ran toward the noise. He reached for his weapon as he ran, only to find it wasn't there.

He wasn't wearing his shoulder harness or his uniform. *Damn it!*

Slowing because he was unarmed, he questioned whether he should retreat to the house.

Two horses, their reins trailing, thundered past him as he stood frozen with indecision.

Where's Jake?

If his brother let the horses run off without their riders, something had to be wrong.

More gunshots resounded, and Dillon shook off the uncertainty, racing toward the direction they hailed from.

But he fell over something on his way.

Scrambling to his feet, he stared down at what had tripped him. It was Officer Spence.

The young man's eyes were open, but he stared at nothing. Dillon crouched down and noticed the blood covering the officer's white uniform shirt. He'd taken two shots to the chest.

Knowing there wouldn't be one, Dillon felt for a pulse. But Spence was dead.

Because I hesitated.

Dillon closed the young man's eyes and stood. Then he squeezed his own lids shut, trying to block out the sight that haunted him.

When he opened them, the ceiling of his bedroom loomed above him. Shadows from the fan blades danced across the boards where the light from the streetlamp outside his window shone in.

His small apartment was on the top floor of a rehabilitated 1930s hardware store. There was a sandwich shop on the bottom, which suited him just fine because it meant food was never far away. He'd been renting the small one-bedroom dwelling for the last five years.

Realizing how long it'd been, he thought maybe it was

time to buy a place, but he'd miss living right in town. Rolling Brook was small, and the further out you went, the farther you had to travel to get to anything. He preferred being in the thick of things, but he could do without the modern streetlamp shining in his window right now.

It was nearly as tall as the building and the light always seemed to hit right in his bedroom. He'd bought heavy drapes to shut it out but forgotten to close them.

Watching the shadows now, he sighed heavily and unconsciously rubbed his chest in the same spot where Officer Spence had been shot.

That was the second time this week that he'd dreamt about the night Spence had been killed.

Before that night, he'd never lost one of his junior officers. Rolling Brook was usually a sleepy little Midwest town, but now it was marred by violence. Violence he couldn't seem to shake.

Reaching for his phone on the low nightstand beside his bed, he glanced at its clock.

4:30 a.m.

He grimaced. Well, it was going to be an early start for him today. Rolling out of bed, he stumbled to the ensuite shower. Turning the water on fullly hot, he wished it would wash away the memory of losing Officer Spence.

CHAPTER 1

Dillon

Jameson knocked on Dillon's office door. The man was built like a Celtic warrior, and his large hand managed to rattle the entire frame.

"Hey, Redland, Captain wants to see ya." As usual, files were scattered over Dillon's desk, and he had more piles of them strategically arranged on the floor. "You know you have a filing cabinet, right?"

"That's Lieutenant Redland, Sergeant Jameson," Dillon smirked at his redheaded friend and avoided the filing cabinet comment.

He knew he had one, he just found it easier to find things when they were spread out in front of him. He also knew Jameson had purposely left out his title to rag him. He enjoyed returning the favor by correcting the sergeant. They'd grown up together and been on the police force for nearly the same number of years. Dillon had just gotten luckier on the promotion front. Although at times like this, when he had to deal with the captain, he wasn't so sure he was the lucky one.

"Did he say what he wants?" Dillon scratched at his dark head. It'd been a while since he'd gotten a haircut, and his usual buzzcut had grown out.

Can't be good if he wants me specifically.

What had he messed up now?

"Nope. Good luck." Jameson winked at him and walked away.

Staring after his friend, Dillon sighed. He wasn't fond of the captain, but the feeling was mutual. He tried to stay out of the man's crosshairs as much as possible. Every time they had to interact, one or both of them ended up shouting. Well, usually, *he* was the one getting shouted at.

He'd love to shout back, but Dillon respected rank and didn't want to jeopardize his position on the force. Police work was too important to him.

Growing up, he'd always known he wanted to help people. When he'd completed that first class at the police academy twelve years ago, he'd found his calling. He'd thought about joining the force in Chicago, but it had never felt right.

Rolling Brook was small, but it had a decent-sized police department. There were twenty other officers besides himself. The fact there'd been room for growth was one of the reasons he'd stayed. Otherwise, he probably would have ended up in Chicago like his brother had. Even his sister had left town when she'd gone off to college. But they had both come back; Rolling Brook was in their blood.

Redlands had lived in Rolling Brook for as long as the

town existed, maybe even before. His ancestors had married into the Cahokia tribe and settled just outside the limits, establishing Whiteford Farm—the same one his brother owned now.

He'd been glad when Jake wanted the farm. Dillon loved his family and the property—it was 10,000 acres of crop fields, cattle grazing lands, and a lake that he still enjoyed swimming in during the summer—but he'd never enjoyed the work that went into running it. Not the way Jake did.

He'd rather protect people, not cows.

Shaking his head at the thought, Dillon knocked on the captain's office door and hoped whatever the man wanted to see him about wouldn't make him regret that fact.

Worrying about it, he tried reminding himself that captains came and went. All he had to do was wait this one out. Hell, he'd try for the position himself in a few years.

Smiling now, he addressed his superior. "Sir, you wanted to see me?"

Captain Grouse looked up from his paperwork with a scowl that made his jowls more prominent. His dark eyes flashed at Dillon. "Come in and shut the door."

Dillon's smile stayed in place, but his jaw clenched. A closed door didn't bode well for him. He shut it, then hovered by the captain's desk, knowing he'd get reprimanded if he sat down before being invited.

Papers overflowed the desk's surface, and though he was hardly one to scoff at another's lack of organizational skills, the mess made him want to cringe. How the man managed to run the department at all with a desk that looked like that, he'd never know.

The captain waved him into a chair, and several papers nearly took flight.

"Sit down, sit down. I don't have all day. I've got the chief's office calling me every five minutes and the county up my ass." Captain Grouse dug through the pile and handed Dillon a letter from the Dale County Sherriff Office's Employee Assistance Program.

"What's this, Captain?"

"You've got to do it, Redland. This is coming down from headquarters. They're all up in arms about the shooting at your brother's farm. Callin' it a critical incident and claiming it requires a debrief and counseling sessions."

Dillon scanned the letter and noted no particular officer was named in the request. It only claimed the department had to show it was following proper methods by providing effective Critical Incident Stress Management through counseling. Man, they even had an acronym for it—CISM.

He glanced back up at the captain. "Why me? There were other officers on the scene."

"Because you were the senior man. Losing Officer Spence was on your watch, Lieutenant. If anyone should go to counseling over this, it ought to be you." The captain crossed his arms over his paunch and leaned back in his chair. "Are you questioning my decision?"

"No, sir. But why's it taken them so long to tell us this? The shooting was three months ago." He'd never heard of CISM, but then, there hadn't been a shooting in Rolling Brook since he'd joined the force ten years ago.

That kind of excitement didn't usually reach this far west of Chicago, but his soon-to-be sister-in-law had unwittingly brought it with her.

Dillon had a moment of panic at the thought of the wedding. He was supposed to do "best man" stuff for his brother, but his job left little time. August couldn't come soon enough for him so he could relinquish those duties.

"Because that's how slow bureaucracy works." Captain Grouse slammed his beefy hand down on his desk, and the whole thing rattled.

Dillon sighed and put thoughts of the wedding aside to focus on what the captain was saying. Clearly, he'd managed to rile the man up again.

"The therapist's information is in the letter. Call her immediately so I can report we're complying with the county's request."

"Yes, sir."

Captain Grouse nodded at him, and Dillon rose, knowing the only way to calm the captain down was to do what he asked.

He left the captain's door open and walked back to his office through the bullpen. The smell of stale coffee assaulted his nose as he passed through, and a couple of rookies made jokes about him getting called to the boss's office—again. He ignored them, focusing on the fact he'd just been ordered to submit to counseling.

Glancing down at the letter, he noted the therapist's name was Doctor Lydia Mason. He was going to do a little digging before he called her office.

Half an hour later, he'd learned very little. The doctor had a surprisingly small online footprint. He'd discovered she'd opened her practice in the county seat just under a year ago. She had several fancy letters after her name but no last known address.

He found that odd.

Just who is Lydia Mason?

Her bio claimed she was thirty-one, but there were no pictures of her to be found. He wanted to know more about the woman if he was supposed to spill his guts to her. Not that he would.

Dillon wasn't going to tell her any more than he had to. Sure, she'd want to know about the night of the shooting, and he could tell her that. He'd had to type it all up in a report, hadn't he? What he wouldn't tell her were the dreams he kept having about it.

Shaking off that thought, Dillon made the call.

"Hello, Dr. Mason's office. My name is Tanya. How can I help you?"

"Hi, Tanya. This is Lieutenant Redland from the Rolling Brook Police Department. I've been ordered, uh, that is, asked to set up a counseling session with Dr. Mason. Is she in?" He winced at his lack of tact. He hadn't meant to say he was *ordered* to see the doctor.

"Oh!" Tanya exclaimed. "Doctor Mason has been expecting your call. She's with a client, but I can set up the session for you. When would you like to come in?"

"As soon as she has an opening available, please." He wanted to get the mandatory counseling over with so the captain wouldn't come breathing down his neck.

"Let's see, Doctor Mason can see you tomorrow at three o'clock. Does that work for you?"

"Sure. Tomorrow at three is great." Dillon scrubbed at

his chin—his five o'clock shadow was starting to show—and tried to think if he had anything already scheduled.

"All right, Lieutenant. I've got you on her schedule. Do you need directions to the office?"

"No, I have the address already." In fact, he was staring at the building on his computer screen. That much he'd been able to find.

"Great! We'll see you tomorrow afternoon."

"Thank you. See you tomorrow." Dillon disconnected and started searching his office for the file on the shooting that ended in the death of Officer Nathan Spence.

* * * *

Lydia

Of course, he had to be handsome. Lydia worked to keep her expression neutral as she stared at the cop hovering in her doorway. He was tall and trim, with dark hair, chiseled features, and arresting blue eyes. Their color was made more apparent by the way they contrasted against his darkly tanned skin. He wore a white button-down shirt rolled up at the sleeves and tucked into a pair of jeans with a belt that held his badge and gun. Though simple, the clothes suited him. She imagined he was the type to wear the uniform as little as possible.

"This is Lieutenant Redland, Doctor," Tanya announced, her blonde curls bouncing as she gestured at the cop. "You go on in, now."

"Thank you, Tanya." Lydia smiled and waited for her perky receptionist to shut the door.

Once she did, Lydia stepped around her desk and offered her hand. "Doctor Mason. It's nice to meet you, Lieutenant."

"Call me Dillon, please." He took her hand and shook it gently.

Wow, the man had huge hands. She caught herself staring down at them. Sidetracked, she had to chide herself to focus and do her job.

"And you can call me Lydia. Please"—she gestured to the couch across from her desk—"have a seat."

Dillon stuck his hands in his pockets and glanced at the sleek, armless sofa. "Uh, I don't suppose you have a chair?"

Despite being in a historic building, she'd furnished her office modernly. Every piece of furniture, from the gray sofa to the bookshelves behind her walnut desk, was midcentury in style. The shelves were smooth and shiny, with no sign of clutter or personal items anywhere, for good reason, but one she didn't like to dwell on.

She forced a chuckle. "Sorry, no. Relax, Lieutenant. I'm not asking you to lie down on it."

Oh crap, that came out wrong!

He glanced at her sidelong, and she was sure he thought she was flirting with him.

"Right," was all Dillon said as he sat down on the edge of the couch.

Well, this is off to a great start. Sarcasm colored the thought.

She struggled to keep her smile in place as she sat down. "Thank you for coming in today. I understand you took part in a critical incident recently. Conducting a debriefing with a certified counselor is part of the stress management process."

When he nodded, she continued, "I am certified to act as a debriefer. I've served in this role with the Chicago P.D. several times."

His only response was to stare at her.

Lydia folded her hands together on her desk. "I want you to know that my office is a supportive, nonjudgmental space and that whatever you say here is confidential."

"Is it, though?" His skepticism was evident on his face.

Despite it, she was happy to have finally elicited a response. "Yes, unless you demonstrate that you are a danger to yourself or others." She resumed as he frowned at her, "I've been informed of the incident that brought you in here, but I want you to tell me what happened in your own words."

His sigh was heavy enough that she heard it across the room.

"Whenever you're ready," she prompted, reaching for her pen and notepad.

"I was already on my way to my brother's house when I heard Officer Spence requesting backup over the radio. He was stationed at the farm as a precaution. That's Whiteford Farm—my brother's property. We had reason to suspect someone was after Blair O'Rourke, who was staying with my brother at the time."

Dillon paused, and she scribbled furiously, noting his clinical recitation of the event.

"Spence reported a lone shooter firing at two civilians on horseback. My brother and Blair," he clarified, though she already knew who the target had been.

"And then what happened?" she asked, glancing up from her notes.

"His transmission cut short. I think I knew then the shooter had gotten him." Dillon grimaced.

"What happened when you arrived on the scene?" She tried not to respond to the grief in his eyes. Something told her the Lieutenant wouldn't appreciate her pointing it out, though she'd have to when he finished relaying the incident, whether he was ready to hear it or not.

His hands clenched into fists, and she noted down his anger. "I saw the shooter running away through the light from my headlamps. I pursued him on foot, but he had a car stashed. After the shooter got away, I went to check on Officer Spence. That's when I found him. He'd sustained two shots to the chest. By the time I got there, he was already gone."

"And what went through your mind when you found him?" Lydia gently asked while she recorded the way he rubbed his chest when explaining about Officer Spence's wounds.

His expression became guarded. "Not sure I remember, Doc. It was a charged situation."

"Hmm," she hummed noncommittally. "Shock and even denial are normal first reactions in those types of situations."

"Maybe." He shrugged.

Great, he's about as ready to talk about his feelings as a French mime.

"Can you tell me what the worst part of the incident was

for you?" She tried to pull more information about the Lieutenant's emotional state since he wasn't giving her much to go on.

She was tempted to tap her pen on her pad out of frustration, but it was a bad habit that could set clients off. An involuntary shiver shook her frame, remembering one of her former client's reactions to her tapping. The man had been certifiable, but still.

"Not catching the bastard then and there," he sneered.

Definite anger over the event, Lydia jotted down. "And why was that the worst part for you?"

"Because he had the chance to hurt more people," he told her through clenched teeth.

"Ah." She ignored his frustration and changed tactics. "And what about since the incident? What have you been experiencing?"

His shoulders went stiff. "I'm not sure what you mean, Doc. The incident is resolved. Thankfully, we caught the man that killed Spence and the people he worked with. They're all being held accountable for his crimes."

"Did you know Officer Spence well, Lieutenant?"

"I asked you to call me Dillon."

She kept her smile easy as he stalled.

"Not really. Spence was just a kid. He'd only been on the force for a year."

"So, he wasn't a close friend?" He shook his head when she asked for clarification. "But you felt responsible for him?" Lydia pushed.

He scrubbed a hand over his face. "Yeah. Is that what you want me to say, Doc? I put him there, didn't I? He was acting on my orders."

"It seems to me, *Dillon*"—she made sure to emphasize his name—"that you are harboring some unresolved anger and guilt over the incident. I'm afraid our time is up for today, but I'm going to recommend to the county that you undergo further sessions to work through those emotions." Finished with her assessment, she snapped her notepad shut and stared him down.

He didn't move, so she waited and watched him struggle to control his anger. He clearly wasn't happy about the idea of further sessions with her. But he needed them.

"You can schedule the next one with Tanya on your way out."

Dillon stood and approached her desk. He'd managed to mask the anger and held his hands up in a gesture of apology. "Look, Lydia, I don't think that's necessary. I'm only here as a formality. The incident is resolved, and it would be best for the town if we drop this and move on." He smiled at her, and she tried not to be charmed by the way it lifted his lip crookedly.

"I understand this session was mandatory for you, Lieutenant, but it is my professional opinion that you have not personally resolved your feelings from the incident."

She knew what that looked like, having dealt with it herself.

"And that is what I will be reporting to the county." Standing, she ushered him toward her office door.

When they reached it, he slammed his hand on the wood before she could open it. Fear spiked within her.

Her face paled, and she listened with wide eyes as he

pleaded, "This is my career on the line, Doctor. I could be taken off cases or even suspended if they think I'm unstable, which is what they will think if I'm going to counseling. You'll ruin my career."

She stood frozen, unable to find the words to tell him to back off. He had only half a foot on her five-foot-seven inches, but right now, it felt like he towered over her. Images of her former client flitted through her mind, and she started to tremble.

He must have noticed because his expression shifted. "Hey, are you okay, Doc?"

When he grabbed her hands, she whimpered. "Please leave." The fear trapped her in its grip and knotted her stomach.

Thankfully, he dropped her hands and stepped away. She could see the questions in his eyes—questions she didn't want to answer. "Leave. Now," was all she managed to get out.

Dillon opened the door, but he turned around after he stepped through. She shut it in his face before he could say anything else, then collapsed against it.

Her body shook as she slid to the floor.

Oh my God. That was ridiculous.

Glancing up at her reflection in the mirror hanging on the wall across the room, Lydia frowned. Her sea-green eyes looked enormous against the current pallor of her face. Tendrils of dark brown hair had escaped her carefully styled chignon and gone frizzy against the perspiration on her usually olive skin.

Why had she reacted that way? Dillon was a cop, for

Pete's sake; he wouldn't hurt her just because he got a little angry. She was going to have to explain things when she saw him again.

Groaning over that fact, she laid her head in her palms.

Way to be professional, Lydia.

CHAPTER 2

Dillon

Dillon drove to Dr. Mason's office at the end of his shift. He'd spent the rest of the afternoon obsessing over her. Sure, his behavior had been unprofessional. He'd let his anger get the better of him, but her reaction continued to worry him.

He'd seen that kind of response before—in women who were victims of domestic abuse. Lydia had been afraid of him; that much was clear.

Who hurt her?

The doctor might be a pain in his professional ass at the moment, but the thought of someone abusing her made his stomach clench. She was both smart and gorgeous. He'd never been attracted to a woman in a blazer before, but the way she'd filled it out and that black pencil skirt . . .

Yeah, he couldn't help but be attracted to her. Of course, he had no plans to take that attraction anywhere. What he *did* plan to do was convince her not to ruin his career with more counseling. But attracted or not, he wouldn't stoop to underhanded methods.

Dillon pulled up in front of the Victorian-era building that had been converted into office space and grimaced. His mood was as gray as the paint on the exterior; he hated that he had to apologize.

Avoiding it for as long as possible, he let his gaze roam over the buildings adjacent to hers. This whole side of the street was a hodgepodge of historic buildings. Two-story brick storefronts were mashed up next to three-story Victorian architecture, complete with clapboard siding and protruding front porch steps.

The pizza place next to her office sounded much more appealing than what he knew he needed to do. His stomach growled in agreement, but he ignored it.

Climbing out of his police cruiser, he hoped his showing up again wouldn't make things worse. He just couldn't let go of the fear he'd seen so clearly written on her face. His detective's brain needed to know why she was afraid, and his cop's heart had to ask if she needed his help.

Grumbling over the fact he had to deal with the whole counseling situation in the first place, he took the stairs to the doctor's second-floor office. The receptionist was gone when he entered. He hoped like hell he hadn't missed Lydia, too. Holding his breath, he knocked and waited.

She opened the door but didn't look happy when she saw it was him on the other side of it. "What brings you back to my office so soon, Lieutenant?"

"Can I come in?" He tried his friendliest smile, hoping she'd make this easier on him.

Moving to her desk, she perched on the edge of it and crossed her arms. He got her message loud and clear.

This wasn't going to be easy. Friendly Dr. Lydia from earlier was not who he was dealing with now.

"Well?" she prompted.

He cleared his throat. "Look, Doc, I don't get angry, or at least, I didn't used to. I'm sorry about what happened in your office earlier. Really." He used his eyes to plead for understanding.

"That may be, Lieutenant, but it doesn't change the facts. You haven't dealt with your emotions regarding the critical incident. Your lashing out at me is merely a symptom of that. I can help you, but you have to let me. My report remains unchanged. You need counseling." She paused as though realizing something. "Of course," she offered, "if you're uncomfortable conducting sessions with me, we can find another counselor."

That made him frown. "That's not it, Doc. It's my job on the line here. My captain will suspend me if you report that I need counseling. The man has it in for me. Plus, it could ruin my career. Marks like that don't come off your record. They'll see it next time I'm up for promotion. And that's nothing compared to what the guys under me will think. How can I have their respect as a superior if they think I'm losing my grip?"

"Perhaps they'll see the guts it takes to admit you need help, and they'll respect you for that. Isn't that what cops do?" Lydia countered. "Get people help when they need it? It's time you did the same for yourself."

He was getting nowhere. "Speaking of getting people

help . . ." He wanted to know if she needed his but hesitated to bring it up, knowing she'd be afraid again.

"Yes?" she asked when he didn't continue.

He sensed she'd relaxed. Her arms were no longer crossed in front of her. Instead, her hands rested on the edge of the desk.

"Earlier, when I got angry at you"—he stepped toward her and watched her tense up—"you were afraid of me. So, I have to ask . . . do you need help? Is there someone who's—"

"I'm fine, Lieutenant," she cut him off, her knuckles had gone white where she gripped the edge of the desk. "This isn't about me."

He hesitated. Pushing her on the issue probably wasn't in his best interest, but he couldn't shake the feeling that she was in trouble. No one had that kind of fear response without reason. He took a step closer, and she paled. Nope, that wasn't a normal response.

"Lydia," he said softly, "you're clearly afraid. I'm not going to hurt you, but someone has. If you're still in danger, I need to know."

His instinct was to reach for her, but he restrained himself, knowing that would only make things worse.

When she continued to stare at him with wide eyes, he explained, "I've seen this before in victims of domestic abuse. If you're in that kind of situation, I can help you. You just have to tell me."

She seemed to shake herself at his mention of domestic abuse. "No, I, I'm not. It's not that." She must have read the disbelief on his face because she added, "I had a, um, bad experience with a former client."

He could tell the admission embarrassed her as she glanced away from his gaze. "Okay" —he nodded for her to continue—"what happened?"

She sighed heavily, but her hands no longer clenched the edge of the desk. Her color was coming back, too.

"He became obsessed with our sessions, with me," she admitted. "His behavior turned possessive. He didn't want me to counsel my other clients. I noticed the signs and ended our sessions, but he started following me, showing up at my office and even at my house. He was so angry with me." She shivered and closed her eyes briefly as though the memory still unsettled her.

"He stalked you," Dillon stated. The vein at his temple pulsed as the anger toward this client brewed within him. Not wanting to scare her again, he worked to control it.

She nodded. "I filed a restraining order against him when he wouldn't stop."

"That's good. That's what I would've advised," Dillon managed to tell her calmly.

"It is," she agreed, "but—"

Oh shit.

Dillon tensed. He didn't think he would like what came after that 'but.'

"He violated it." She paused, and he witnessed her struggle to keep her composure.

This was the part he was dreading. The reason she was so afraid.

"It started with gifts. He'd leave them on my doorstep. I don't know if he meant them as an apology or he thought they would make me let him back in for his sessions." She shook her head. "The court debated over whether this actually violated the order since I couldn't prove that he had been the one to leave them there. But I knew."

Her gaze lifted to his, and the intensity in it made him reach for her hands. She didn't seem to notice as she told him, "One evening after work, I was walking to my car in the garage. I remember being distracted reading an email on my phone. I heard a noise, but it didn't faze me." She sucked in a deep breath before she continued, "It was a busy office building. I figured someone else was doing the same thing I was. Just heading home after work."

Her eyes were far away now, remembering. "He tapped me on the shoulder"—she flinched, and Dillon gave her hands a gentle squeeze in reassurance—"and I remember spinning around but then I just froze. I don't know why, but I was shocked. He grabbed my arm and started dragging me behind him. I didn't know where he was taking me, and I was too stunned to scream until"—her hands trembled against his palms—"he hit me."

At that, Dillon's fingers unconsciously tightened on hers, and she cried out. Cursing at himself, he dropped her hands.

She stared at him with wild eyes; fear raced through the hazel depths.

Lifting his hands and holding them palms up, he backed away. When he did, her rapid breathing began to slow. "I'm sorry."

Her stare went through him, and she hugged her arms across her chest. "I know."

His voice strained when he asked, "What happened after he hit you, Lydia?"

"He meant to knock me unconscious, I think. We'd reached his car, and he opened the trunk." Lydia shuddered and closed her eyes.

He could imagine the thoughts that had to have run through her mind at that moment.

"It knocked me down, the punch, but I wasn't out. I started screaming and kicking at him. Thank God someone saw and came to my aid. I don't even remember the person. It's just a blur after that"—she shook her head—"waiting for the police, the hospital." She opened her eyes and focused on him.

Dillon was glad to see they were clear now.

"They sent him to jail for violating the order. He got the maximum sentence, 364 days. That was a year ago today."

"And that's why you're so on edge." Understanding settled over him. Other things started to fall into place, the reason she'd moved to Rolling Brook and even . . .

"So, what's your real name, Doctor?" He smiled to try and lighten the mood.

She returned his smile wanly, but at least it wasn't a frown. "It is Lydia, but it's Lydia Pallas—my father's Greek. Mason was my mother's maiden name. I changed it legally. I thought, or hoped, it would be safer."

He kept his smile in place to reassure her. "That's smart, Doc. In this case, it can't hurt to make yourself harder to find."

"I had the order against him extended, too. I just—" She shrugged. "I guess it's been on my mind a lot today, and your reaction earlier brought everything back."

"I truly am sorry about that." He winced. Not only had he brought back bad memories for her, but he'd forced her to share them with him. It seemed only fair to do the same.

"You're right, you know"—he glanced away from her—"about the incident. I can't . . . I haven't let it go."

She surprised him by laying a hand on his arm. "Let me help you, Dillon." Her voice was soft as she told him, "I've seen what can happen if you don't get treatment. There were cops I worked with in Chicago who lost not only their careers but their families, too because they needed help and never asked for it. You're worried about the counseling ruining your career, but not getting help could ruin it all the same." Her eyes pleaded with him, and he found himself wanting to give in to them, to let himself sink into their ocean-colored depths.

His phone rang and interrupted his errant thoughts. Breaking her gaze, he glanced at the screen. "I have to take this," he explained as he walked to the door. "I'll be in touch, Doc."

"Wait—"

"Redland," Dillon answered his phone and waved at her as he left. He had to get out of there before Lydia had a chance to argue, or he had a chance to do something he'd regret.

CHAPTER 3

Dillon

Dillon's eyes stared at his computer screen, but his mind wasn't focused on the words written there. He'd managed to get through a full day of work without thinking about Lydia.

Though now, his thoughts drifted to her and everything she'd told him the evening before. He mentally kicked himself for not asking for more information about her stalker.

Last night, he hadn't wanted to upset her more than he already had, but if he'd gotten a name, he could have looked the bastard up.

Dillon grimaced. If it worried him that the man was released, he could only imagine what Lydia must be going through. He had the urge to call her to see how she was doing. Maybe he could casually get the guy's name out of her.

Hell, who was he kidding? There was nothing casual

about his thoughts. He'd spent half the night thinking about her despite the fact the captain was likely going to suspend him *because* of her.

It had been a pleasant way to fill his time when the insomnia kicked in. He hadn't even dreamt about Officer Spence last night.

Thinking of him now, Dillon unconsciously rubbed his chest. He'd have to call her eventually, or she'd likely call him to set up his next counseling session.

A sudden thought made him grin. He had a very particular idea of what their next session could entail, and it didn't involve talking.

His phone rang, and he cleared his throat to answer it. "Hi, Doc." Either Lydia was psychic and appalled by the turn of his thoughts, or she was calling him because of his hasty exit the night before. "Look, I know. I'm going to schedule—"

"Dillon," she interrupted him on a gasp, and he picked up on the fear in her voice.

"What is it? What's wrong?" He was instantly alert. The seconds it took for her to answer were agonizing.

"He's back. Oh my god, he's back. The gifts, he left me a gift—" Her voice broke into a sob.

"Okay, it's going to be okay, Lydia. Where are you? Are you alone?" He needed to know that the stalker wasn't with her, but he didn't want her alone.

"At home. I'm at home. It was on my doorstep when I got here," she managed to tell him through the tremor of tears in her voice.

"All right, stay put. I'm coming over. What's your

address?" Dillon shoved to his feet and was already halfway to the station door before she gave it to him.

"I want you to do something for me, okay? I need you to double-check all your doors and windows. Make sure they're locked. Can you do that?" He hoped giving her a task to focus on would keep her from panicking.

"Yes, I will."

A measure of relief trickled through the tension when she sounded more in control.

"Great, I'll be right there." He expected her to hang up as he unlocked his police cruiser.

"Dillon, thank you. I . . ."

He waited for her to say something more until it was apparent that she wasn't going to. "I'm on my way, Lydia."

He hung up and gunned it out of the parking lot.

* * * *

Lydia

After her call to Dillon, Lydia calmed down enough to be embarrassed by how she'd sobbed in his ear. He probably thought she was some weepy female who would dissolve into hysterics.

She'd have to show him that was not the case.

Determined to keep her cool, she splashed water on her face and glanced in the bathroom mirror. She grimaced at her reflection. It was apparent she'd lost control. Her eyes were puffy, and the tip of her nose was red from crying.

She knew she was focusing on her appearance instead of thinking about the fact that her stalker was back.

Classic denial.

After rolling her eyes at herself, she fixed what little she could with makeup but didn't have time for much more than that. Dillon would be there any minute.

Thank God. She closed her eyes on an exhale of relief.

When she'd seen that blue box on her steps, she'd nearly fainted. Luckily, the fear of Samuel being behind her had pulled her out of it. He hadn't been, but she'd definitely hastened inside. She hadn't even picked up the box. It was still sitting there, taunting her.

Opening her eyes, she counseled her reflection, "You need to deal with your past trauma." With a sigh, she shook her head. It was easier to tell someone else what to do. Harder to take your own advice.

Moving to Rolling Brook was supposed to be a fresh start, but the remarkable calm she'd felt when she'd found this place was tainted now. She'd thought she'd be safe leaving the city, and her heart had leaped at the site of the red brick bungalow.

Without a second thought, she'd put an offer in, thinking it was fate that she'd found a house so easily. After years of living in apartments in Chicago, she'd perhaps been overly eager. She should have gone farther away, made it harder for him to find her.

Trying not to dwell on it, she checked all the doors and windows as Dillon requested. They'd been locked when she'd left for work. It had become part of her routine ever since the incident with Samuel.

She checked them every day, even when he'd been in prison. Her breath hitched at the thought that he wasn't anymore. Thankfully, the sound of a police siren kept her from panicking, and she moved to look out the window of her front door.

Dillon got out of the police cruiser with his gun raised. He scanned the street and her front yard with it before making a circuit of the house.

Her eyes stayed glued to the white cruiser with 'Rolling Brook Police' emblazoned on the side in bright blue as she waited for him to return. She knew he was looking for Samuel but didn't think her stalker was still there.

At least that wasn't what he'd done before. It had been weeks of gifts before he'd tried to abduct her.

It didn't take long before Dillon was back. She let out a huge breath, relieved that he'd put his gun away.

Samuel's not here, then.

Dillon climbed the steps to her porch and picked up the gift. Turning it over, he examined it—for what, she wasn't sure. Wanting to get this over with, she opened her door.

"Hi." Her eyes were instinctively drawn to the box in his hands.

"Can I come in?" When he asked, she realized she was standing in the doorway staring like an idiot.

"Of course," she offered as she stepped back to let him in, "thank you for coming."

As soon as Dillon was inside, she turned and locked the heavy wooden door. Her thoughts were jumbled, and she wasn't sure where to start.

Thankfully, he took the lead. "How are you?"

That wasn't what she was expecting him to ask. Surprise made her meet his deep blue eyes. She suddenly wished he would hold her; she wanted comfort, and no one had held her in over a year.

Her last boyfriend had broken up with her over the Samuel thing. He'd had the nerve to think she'd encouraged the gifts, and she'd quickly realized she didn't need that in her life.

Lydia sighed at her train of thought. What she needed was to focus on how to deal with Samuel being back instead of wallowing in past hurts.

"Shaken?" She shrugged. "But better than when I called you earlier." That wasn't exactly the truth, but she was determined to make it so. "What are you going to do with that?" She pointed at the small blue box he still held.

It was neatly wrapped and tied with a white satin bow, exactly like all the previous gifts she'd received from Samuel.

"I'll take it into the station. If it's from your stalker, it's evidence." She noticed him glance around and tried not to roll her eyes at herself. They were still standing in her foyer.

"Did you want to sit down?"

When he nodded, she gestured him toward the living room. It wasn't far since her bungalow was tiny compared to a modern home. It had been built in the 1920s and still boasted the same footprint with narrow halls and cozy rooms.

He paused at the entryway to the living room and turned to her with a half-smile. "You're not really into chairs, are ya?"

She gazed at the matching couches she'd inherited with the house. They were a deep purple velvet with rounded backs that tapered into piped arms. Coming from a small apartment in the city, she'd been glad of the extra furniture. They were eclectic, but she liked that about them. Maybe she wouldn't have bought them herself, but they fit the room.

It was large for an older house and probably her favorite simply because it had a gorgeous tile fireplace with matching craftsman bookcases flanking it. She'd thoughtfully arranged her shelves with books and décor— no sign of clutter or disarray.

Like her office, some might call them sparse, but she preferred the term clean. Besides, she had an issue with knickknacks. They made her sad since they reminded her of her mother, who had always seemed to fill every available surface with them.

Still gazing at her living room, lost in thought, Lydia noticed for the first time that the tiles around the fireplace had purple flecks, which matched the couches.

Dillon cleared his throat and brought her attention back to his question.

"Huh, guess not." She tried to smile at him, but it wobbled a little.

He sat on the couch opposite the one she'd taken and took out a small notepad from the chest pocket of his uniform shirt. The bright white of the shirt was a sharp contrast to the deep copper of his skin. Its sleeves were short, and Lydia stared at his biceps, which strained against the fabric as he scratched at his five o'clock shadow.

"Start from the beginning and tell me what happened,"

he instructed as he turned his piercing blue eyes on her.

Watching him now, it occurred to her their roles had reversed. He was the one asking questions and taking notes.

She took a deep breath; she needed to focus. "There's not much to tell. I got home and found the package on my porch. It—"

"What time?" he interrupted her.

"Sorry?" His abrupt question threw her addled brain off track.

"What time did you get home?"

"Oh. Um, I think it was about five-thirty. I left the office a few minutes after five since I didn't have an evening session today."

"You called me at five twenty-three." He told her matter-of-factly. "What happened after you found the package?"

"I," Lydia paused. She didn't want to tell him she'd nearly fainted out of terror. "It was already there, as I mentioned on the phone. I didn't touch it. I couldn't." She shivered. "I went inside and called you right after I saw it."

"Did you notice anything out of the ordinary? Was anything out of place?"

She shook her head in answer.

"What about other people? Were any of your neighbors outside when you got home? Or did you see anyone in the neighborhood you didn't recognize?"

She understood where he was going with this. "No, it was quiet. No one was outside. I didn't see him or anyone else."

"That's okay. I can still canvas the neighborhood and

find out if anyone else noticed someone visiting your house."

That was standard procedure, but she didn't need the confirmation. She had no doubt the package came from Samuel.

"Why do you think the package is from the stalker?"

She tried not to be offended by his question. He was only doing his job, but having the police not believe her about the gifts was something she'd already had to deal with.

"It's exactly like the others he gave me before . . . before he tried to abduct me." She took a calming breath when her voice wanted to wobble. "It's the same wrapping paper and the same bow."

He looked up from his notepad, and the intensity of his eyes struck her. "If you think it's from the stalker, I believe you, Lydia. I want you to know that."

"Thank you." She felt relief that he believed her but wondered if there was more to it. She'd thought she'd seen something deeper in his eyes.

"What's his name? The stalker?"

She shook herself.

No, he's just doing his job.

"Samuel. Samuel Owens."

Dillon nodded. "Okay. I'll see if we can find him for questioning. In the meantime, do you have someone you can stay with? Or that could stay with you? It's best not to be alone if he's stalking you again."

She shook her head. "I have family, but they don't live close."

He frowned at her. "What about a significant other? Or a friend?"

"My last boyfriend broke up with me over this." She didn't care for the expression of sympathy on his face. "I'll be fine, Lieutenant. Everything is locked up tight for the night, and I can ride to work in the morning with Tanya." She could tell he was about to argue. "Look, Dillon, finding that package spooked me. I'll admit that, but I can't live my life in fear of Samuel." As tough as she sounded, she hoped she could live up to her words.

He sighed. "Okay, but don't hesitate to call me if something else happens."

"I won't." When she rose, he followed her to the door.

"I'll let you know as soon as I find out anything." He hesitated as though he wanted to say more.

Lydia looked up, confused, until she saw the expression on his face. The raw need there surprised her and made her pulse race.

She had no idea he felt that way for her, and the thought of kissing him was intriguing. Glancing at his mouth, she sighed. She couldn't let it happen. He was her client. Any relationship outside that was out of the question, at least for now.

She was about to step away when Dillon crushed her against him. His lips sought hers, and his tongue demanded entry.

When she gasped, he took advantage, kissing her deeper and rougher than she'd ever experienced.

She surprised herself by enjoying it. Her body responded in all the right ways, and as he continued to kiss her brains out, she lost track of time. He could have been devouring her for ten seconds or ten minutes.

She had no idea why, but there was a reason they had to stop.

When she moaned, his head snapped up. His eyes were wild, as if he feared what had just happened.

"That was a bad idea." He pulled away from her, and satisfaction filled her to see his breathing was as heavy as hers.

"Yes." She nodded. There was a reason it was a bad idea, but she was still trying to remember what that was.

Staring at Dillon's chiseled face, she attempted to collect her thoughts. His features distracted her, though. Those cheekbones were extraordinary, and his pupils . . . electric.

He shifted under her gaze, and her eyes caught the blue of Samuel's gift.

Seeing it, she cringed. The thought of her stalker cleared the desire that had clouded her brain.

"Dillon, that was . . .," she paused, unsure she could describe that kiss. Clearing her throat, she got to the point. "We can't have anything outside of a professional relationship. Not while I'm counseling you."

There, she'd said it.

He stared at her for several seconds while she couldn't read his expression. "Unless you weren't counseling me."

Oh! Of all the dick moves . . .

"Is that what that kiss was, Lieutenant? A last-ditch effort to change my report on you?" Her voice was low but sharp. The outrage over his using her was bubbling close to the surface.

Seeing the shock on his face, she second-guessed her assumption.

"No. That's not what I . . ." He cleared his throat. "Look, that came out wrong. I just meant"—he scrubbed a hand across his face—"hell, I don't know what I meant. I'm sorry." He paused, "I am attracted to you."

The heat in his gaze was definitely not fake; she could almost feel it scorching her.

"But that crossed a line." He rubbed the back of his neck. "I should go. I'll update you tomorrow about Samuel."

She opened the door but stopped him from leaving with a hand on his arm. "Thank you for coming over. I needed your help, Dillon. Just like you need mine."

She needed him to accept that if she was going to assist him in moving past the loss of Officer Spence.

He didn't shrug her hand off, but his expression was hardly friendly. "We'll talk tomorrow. Don't forget to call Tanya about a ride to work."

"I won't. Goodnight, Lieutenant."

When he nodded, she shut the door. Knowing he'd probably wait to leave until he heard it click, she turned the lock.

As she watched him walk away, she wished she'd thrown her ethics out the window and asked him to stay. She would have regretted it, of course. But if the kiss was any indication, what a night that would have been.

She fanned herself and smirked—until she remembered Samuel.

Thinking about her stalker made her wish she'd asked

Dillon to stay simply because she didn't want to be alone. She frowned, aggravated with herself. She'd meant what she'd said to Dillon. Living her life in fear of Samuel was not an option. She was strong, and she could handle this.

Grabbing her phone, she dialed Tanya's number. Hopefully, her receptionist wouldn't mind picking her up because she had no one else to call.

I really need to make some friends here.

* * * *

Samuel

Samuel threw his empty whiskey glass against the wall of his luxury hotel room and watched it shatter.

She hadn't accepted his gift.

It was supposed to be a reminder of what they'd shared. Lydia should have been happy to receive it, but no, she'd let that cop take it.

He hated cops. They'd taken Lydia away from him.

Samuel growled. He'd had enough of them over the last year.

As soon as he'd gotten out of prison, he'd had to see her again. He was even glad she'd left Chicago. That had to mean she was listening to him and not taking other clients anymore.

The thought calmed him, and he bent to pick up the broken glass. He would try again.

Surely, his next gift would make Lydia see reason. They had sessions to continue after all.

CHAPTER 4

Dillon

As usual, Dillon hadn't slept, but this time, it wasn't dreaming about losing Spence that kept him awake. It had been thoughts of the way he'd left things with Lydia. He wasn't surprised that he'd kissed her. Hell, he'd been thinking about doing it for twenty-four hours straight.

No, what troubled him was that he'd tried to use it to his advantage. He hadn't meant to, but the words had come out somehow. Thinking about it now made him cringe. He hardly recognized himself.

Is this what she'd meant about losing more than my job?

Dillon frowned. He was beginning to think that Lydia was right—maybe he did need her help.

Cursing about that, he shoved to his feet and started pacing within the confines of his office. He needed to stop berating himself over the kiss and focus on the real problem—her stalker.

After leaving her house the night before, he'd returned

to the station and called Chicago. The police department there had gone to check on Owens at Dillon's request but with no luck. The man hadn't been home.

This hadn't come as a surprise to Dillon. It was more than likely the stalker was close by after leaving the gift on Lydia's doorstep. Of course, that didn't make him feel any better about her living alone.

His hands clenched into fists as he paced. He'd called all the places someone could stay at while in town, and it was clear Owens wasn't in Rolling Brook. Dillon had officers looking further afield in the neighboring towns. Still, his gut told him the stalker wouldn't be easy to find.

Canvassing her neighborhood hadn't provided any new information either. No one had seen anything. The area where Lydia lived was old—safe, quiet.

None of her neighbors had video cameras that could have provided footage of the gift being delivered. Neither did Lydia, but he was going to suggest that she install some form of surveillance.

Not only had no one seen Owens leave the gift, but his fingerprints hadn't been on it either—not the wrapping paper or the ribbon.

After spending a day and a half on the stalker, he had little new information to give Lydia and no proof it was Owens.

Frustrated, he kicked his filing cabinet and cursed as it sent file folders scattering to the floor. Just what he needed—more work for himself. If he'd put the damn things in there correctly instead of sticking out at all angles, that wouldn't have happened. Grumbling, Dillon bent to pick up the files.

Jameson knocked on the doorframe to his office and startled him. He glanced up from where he crouched on the floor in pursuit of the folders.

"Lieutenant, Captain wants to see you." Jameson's voice had none of its usual joviality, and Dillon didn't miss that he'd used his title.

Standing, he frowned at his friend. "That good, huh, that you're calling me Lieutenant?" He figured he knew what the captain wanted to tell him.

Jameson swallowed. "Yeah, Dill, it's not good."

Dillon nodded. So this was it. He was getting suspended.

"James, I need you to do something for me." He grabbed the file on Lydia's stalker from his desk and handed it to Jameson. "I just got this stalker case. Patrol is chasing down leads. I'll let them know to report to you."

Jameson started to reach for the file but hesitated. "Sure, but—"

Dillon shoved it into his hands. "Take it. The woman . . . is a friend." He cleared his throat. "This case is important to me. I want to know it's being looked into."

Jameson raised an eyebrow at him but nodded.

Dillon reached up, clapped him on the shoulder in wordless thanks, then headed to the captain's office.

The door was open, and his superior looked up before he could knock on the frame.

"Come in and close the door," Captain Grouse told him with a smile.

Dillon wasn't sure he'd ever seen the captain smile. At

least not when talking to *him*—if Dillon had needed more reason to think he was getting suspended, that would've done it.

He stepped inside and closed the door as instructed. "Sir, you wanted to see me?"

The captain's smile grew. "Seems the county has requested you undergo more sessions with the therapist."

He nodded down at the man. The fact the captain hadn't asked him to sit wasn't lost on Dillon. "Yes, sir. I understood that was going to be her recommendation."

Now, Captain Grouse frowned. "And you don't think you should've told me that?"

Dillon silently cursed himself. He hadn't needed to reveal that fact. "I apologize, sir, but I thought that was privileged information."

The captain smiled again. His eyes gleamed as though Dillon had told him exactly what he'd wanted to hear. "Well, clearly it wasn't. I'm afraid, in light of this, I'm going to have to suspend you, Lieutenant. Turn in your badge and your weapon."

He unholstered his gun, removed his badge from the clip on his waist, and laid them on the captain's desk. "For how long, sir?"

"That depends on you, Lieutenant. As soon as the therapist clears you, we'll reconsider your duties."

Fuck! Dillon swallowed around the bile surging up his throat.

He'd known he would get suspended, which could hurt his future career, but he hadn't thought it would affect his current status. The captain's words about reconsidering his duties were like a punch in the gut.

Captain Grouse wasn't done. "Jameson will take over whatever you're working on. Conduct turnover with him and then get yourself to the counselor."

"Yes, sir. About the counselor—I'm actually working on a case involving her. She's had an issue with one of her clients stalking her." He wanted to bring the captain up to speed on it lest he accuse him of withholding information again.

"What? She's got a stalker?" The captain's tone revealed his anger at the information, and his delighted smile vanished. "What happened?"

A part of Dillon was glad to have stolen the man's glee at suspending him, no matter how petty it was. "She came home to find a gift on her doorstep. It's similar to the ones she received before from the client who was stalking her and—"

"She receives a gift, and suddenly it's from a stalker?" Captain Grouse cut him off. "That's not enough to go on, and you know it, Redland," he told Dillon as he shook his head. The movement caused the captain's combover to shift, and he patted it back into place.

Dillon clenched his fists. "Sir—"

"No. It's not enough. We can't do anything at this stage. I hope you told her that."

"But, sir—"

The captain slammed his fists onto his desk and pointed toward the door. "Out of my office, Redland."

He ground his teeth together. His hands were shaking with the urge to punch the captain in his smug face.

"Out!" Captain Grouse yelled at him.

Dillon wrenched the man's door open and slammed it behind him as hard as he could. He was seething, and his pulse pounded in his ears.

Caught in a rage-filled haze, he punched a hole in the wall outside the captain's office. Unaware of the stares from the bullpen or the blood on his knuckles, Dillon walked out of the police station.

* * * *

Dillon

Dillon found himself parked in front of Lydia's office building, though the drive over was a blur. Realizing his hands were clenched so hard around the steering wheel that his knuckles had gone white, he consciously tried to relax them.

Seeing the blood crusting his right hand, he remembered punching the wall. His anger spiked at the memory, and its heat flooded his body. He'd wanted to destroy something—anything—to crush the feeling of helplessness that boiled within him at the thought of being suspended.

How could he keep Lydia safe if he couldn't do his job?

She needed protection, and he couldn't lose her like he'd lost Spence. Dillon grimaced and rubbed at his chest. He couldn't fail like that again—not ever again.

The thought sent his fists back to clenching on the steering wheel. It was her damn fault he'd gotten suspended. She'd robbed him of his badge and weapon, now he could hardly help her.

Furious over that fact, he slammed his way out of the patrol car and stomped up the steps to her building.

He took the stairs to the second floor two at a time and brushed past Tanya's desk without so much as a nod.

At Lydia's closed door, he raised a fist and pounded. "Doc, open up. I need to speak with you."

Tanya jumped up, frantic. "Lieutenant Redland! You can't do that. Sit a moment, and I'll let her know you're here."

He fixed the young woman with a hard stare. "Oh, I think she already knows I'm here, Tanya."

"But—" Tanya didn't get to finish as Lydia jerked her office door open.

"Excuse me, Lieutenant." She glared at him, then turned to the wide-eyed woman perched on the edge of her office couch. "Ms. Cunningham, I'm afraid there's some urgent business I need to attend to. I'm sorry your session was interrupted. If you'd like to wait, we can continue after I've talked to the Lieutenant, or if you'd prefer, you can reschedule with Tanya."

The blonde, middle-aged woman glanced between him and Lydia and rose to her feet. Dillon bared his lip in a snarl and convinced her she should leave. "I'll reschedule, Doctor."

"Thank you, Ms. Cunningham. Again, I apologize for the interruption."

As Ms. Cunningham walked to Tanya's desk, Lydia gestured for him to come in, then shut the door behind him. "What is so important, Lieutenant?"

He paced in front of the couch. When he looked at her, his nostrils flared. "You got me suspended."

She bristled at his tone. "I'm sorry if you were suspended due to my recommendation. But we've been over this. You need counseling."

Her calm put him more on edge, and he snapped at her. "I know that, Doc." He could tell she didn't understand.

"Then why are you so angry?"

"Because if I can't do my job, how am I supposed to keep you safe?" he yelled, and she took an instinctive step back from him. "We've got nothing on Owens, dammit! And now I'm off the case."

He saw her swallow hard, and part of his brain registered the fact he was scaring her, but he couldn't seem to stop. "He's not in Chicago or staying in Rolling Brook. We don't know where he is, and none of your neighbors saw anything."

As he stared Lydia down, his body vibrated with anger. It raged through him while he waited for her to do or say something. When she didn't respond, he started pacing again.

Moments later, he jerked when she laid her hand on his arm. He hadn't noticed her come up to him.

When he turned to look at her, her eyes radiated calm. "Dillon, surely another officer can help with Samuel, and I'm taking precautions." She squeezed his arm reassuringly. "That's not why you're really upset. Will you sit down?"

His anger cooled under her warm gaze. He didn't know if it was from her words or her touch, but he was glad of it.

"Oh! Your hand." He looked down at the hand she'd lifted. It seemed to have stopped bleeding, at least. "Here, I'll ask Tanya for the first-aid kit. Sit down."

This time, Dillon sat. He watched Lydia rush into action and wondered at her ability to calm him down.

What is it about her?

"What happened?" she asked as he let her clean up the scrapes on his knuckles.

"I punched a wall." He shrugged. "It seemed like a good thing to do at the time."

"Better than punching *someone*, I suppose," she muttered. "There," she said louder, "all fixed."

He glanced down and had to smile at the superhero bandages covering his knuckles. He raised an eyebrow at her.

"It was either that or princesses," she chuckled. "Tanya stocked it. She has kids."

"Thanks, Doc." He flexed his fingers. His right hand was sore, but at least he hadn't broken anything.

"So," Lydia began, "want to tell me why you punched a wall?"

He shrugged again. "The captain pissed me off." Remembering he might get demoted, his expression turned sour. "He didn't just suspend me, Lydia. He's probably going to make me ride a desk when I go back—he'll take my command from me."

She hissed a sharp breath, and Dillon was surprised as her sea-green eyes flashed with anger. "They're not supposed to do that! It undermines the stress-management program. This is why cops like you don't get help when they need it. What's his name—your captain? I'll report him to the county."

He appreciated that she wanted to help him, but he didn't think reporting Captain Grouse would do him any favors.

"Maybe it won't come to that. Anyways, I'm here. They want me to do counseling sessions, so counsel me." He wriggled his eyebrows at her, trying to lighten the mood.

"Well, since my last session was cut short—" He sheepishly smiled as she mock-glared at him. "I suppose I can fit you in."

He was glad she could tease him after he'd barged into her office like an angry asshole.

She moved to sit behind her desk, and he tried not to wish she'd stayed beside him on the couch instead. He wasn't sure he was ready to tell Dr. Mason anything, but Lydia . . . *she* was easier to talk to.

Dillon sighed. If he had any chance at getting reinstated, he had to try.

CHAPTER 5

Lydia

Lydia wanted to sigh in frustration when Dillon gave her another non-answer. They'd had three sessions over the last week and a half, including the day he'd barged into her office. Yet, he still hadn't revealed anything meaningful about the trauma he'd experienced.

The man stubbornly refused—at least it seemed to her—to talk about his feelings. She was running out of ideas to get them out of him. For what seemed like the hundredth time, she asked him to tell her how he felt about losing Officer Spence.

When it seemed to her like the silence had stretched into hours, she realized he wasn't going to say anything, so she broke it. "You do that whenever you think of him." She pointed at Dillon's chest. "Rub the spot where Officer Spence was shot."

She didn't think he was even aware of the gesture. Maybe calling him out on it would finally get him to talk.

His frown told her she was right; he didn't know he was doing it.

"Why do you think that is, Doc?"

Great, now he's countering my questions with more questions.

But maybe that was genuine concern in his eyes; perhaps he really did want to know.

"I think it's a coping mechanism for you. Your stress level increases at the thought of what happened to Officer Spence, and the action of rubbing your chest—though committed unconsciously—decreases your anxiety over the memory." She paused, studying his expression, which revealed nothing, before adding, "Coping mechanisms are common among people with post-traumatic stress disorder."

"What? I don't have PTSD."

She'd figured the mention of PTSD would set him off. Looking into his incredulous stare, she hoped it wouldn't cause him to shut down on her again. The idea made her want to scream.

Instead, she told him calmly, "I didn't say that, Lieutenant. But you *have* exhibited some PTSD symptoms, which is common after trauma." Folding her hands in front of herself, she stared him down. "You told me you've had trouble sleeping, and I've witnessed your angry outbursts on more than one occasion. These changes to your normal physical and emotional reactions are symptoms."

Letting that sink in, she watched Dillon closely as she waited for his response. He seemed to be debating some inner conflict, and she tried not to notice how sexy the scruff on his cheek was where his jaw clenched and unclenched.

When he finally spoke, she pulled her eyes back up to his.

"Yeah," he rubbed the back of his neck and admitted, "it's not just trouble sleeping, Doc." He took a deep breath. "I've had dreams . . . about the night it happened."

At his words, she had to stop herself from jumping up and doing a victory lap. She was nearly giddy with success.

Finally, we're getting somewhere!

She worked to keep her voice even over the joy she was feeling. "Thank you for telling me that. How often do you have these dreams? Are they recurring?"

Before he answered, he leaned his head back on her office couch and closed his eyes as if he dreaded the answer he was about to give. "Almost every night. It's always the same dream."

She hummed in reassurance. "Walk me through it."

He let out a long, low sigh before telling her, "I'm at the farm, and I hear gunshots. I head toward the sound, but then I notice I'm unarmed, so I stop . . . I hesitate."

She noted down the almost imperceptible cringe he gave at that.

"I hear more shots, and I start running again until I trip. The thing that trips me is Spence. I know he's dead, but I feel for his pulse anyway. His eyes are staring up at me, and I close them. Then I wake up."

She was nodding at him when he opened his eyes. From their first session, she knew he was harboring guilt over the incident. His dream cemented that fact. What she didn't yet know was why.

"It sounds like you blame yourself for Officer Spence's death. Why is that?"

He dropped his head into his hands and leaned forward with his elbows on his knees. "I shouldn't have sent him there alone. He was just a rookie. If there'd been another cruiser—"

"You might have lost two officers instead of one." She needed him to realize Officer Spence's death wasn't his fault, and wallowing in guilt wouldn't help him.

She came around her desk and grabbed his hands to make him look at her. "Dillon, he might have been a rookie, but you trusted him to do the job. If you hadn't, you wouldn't have put him there in the first place."

When he nodded at her, she spoke softly. "You can't beat yourself up over what-ifs. His death was not your fault."

Dillon stared down at their clasped hands. "Logically, I know that . . ."

"But not emotionally," she said as she squeezed his hands.

He looked up, and the heat in his gaze flooded her with warmth. She dropped his hands as though they'd scalded her and stepped back before she did something crazy—like kiss him.

"I think that's enough for today."

Needing distance from those deep blue eyes, she returned to her desk and sat down.

"Opening up about your dream is a step in the right direction. The more you share with me, the quicker we can get you back on the force."

And off my client list.

If he kept looking at her like that, she was in danger of being unprofessional. Her lips parted at the thought of kissing him again.

As though he could read her mind, Dillon stood and walked toward her. He placed his palms on her desk and leaned down until his face was mere inches from hers.

When his gaze raked over her and lingered on her lips, she swallowed.

"Until next time, Doc." With that, he pushed off her desk and left.

When he'd gone, she exhaled loudly, unaware she'd been holding her breath.

Whoa. You're in trouble, Lydia.

He'd agreed to keep things on a professional level, but she wondered which one of them would cave first.

CHAPTER 6

Dillon

Two days later, Dillon glanced at the clock in the dash as he pulled into the parking lot in front of Lydia's office building and winced. He was ten minutes late for his session.

One of the hotels he'd contacted about the stalker before he'd gotten suspended had called him back with a lead. A man matching Owens's description had checked in that afternoon.

Dillon figured he'd been within his rights as a concerned citizen to follow up on it, but it hadn't panned out. The man wasn't Owens.

He'd already called Jameson to let him know. Now, he had to tell Lydia why he was late.

Grumbling about another dead lead, he climbed out of his SUV. When he turned to head into the building, he saw Lydia rushing in the same direction.

"Hey," he called with a wave as she got closer. "I thought

I was going to be the one to have to apologize for being late." He smiled now, happy with the way things had turned out.

"Oh, hi." She seemed frazzled as she ran her hand over her dark brown hair.

She wore it up in some fancy twist today, and he had the sudden urge to pull the pins out so he could wrap his hands in it. He'd bet her hair smelled as good as it looked. Fighting the temptation, he tucked his hands in his pockets.

"I'm sorry. I was running errands since I had a free hour, and I got held up by one of my neighbors. I ran into her at the market, and she just had to tell me about all the vegetables growing in her garden." Lydia shook her head. "She was complaining that someone trampled through them. It was probably an animal, but on the way here I thought—could it have been Samuel?" Her eyes pinched with worry when she looked up at him.

He hated adding to that worry, but Samuel using her neighbor's yard to sneak up to her house was a possibility. He scratched at the back of his neck and cleared his throat. "Yeah, it could have been him."

She frowned and joined him as they climbed the steps to the front door.

"Look, I had a lead on Owens, but it didn't turn into anything. We're still searching—" He stopped talking at her sharp intake of breath.

"Dillon"—she grabbed ahold of his arm—"look!" She pointed, and he followed her gaze.

Propped against the faded red door to her building was another gift with blue wrapping paper and a white satin bow.

His muscles tensed as his adrenaline kicked into high gear. He was about to search the area for the stalker when her hand slid limply from his arm. Turning, he caught her as she swooned and gently set her down on the steps' landing.

"Lydia! Don't you faint on me!" Dillon demanded as he stared down at her face.

It had gone pale, but when her eyelids fluttered, he relaxed slightly. She wasn't out, not entirely.

"Dillon." Her voice was weak like she'd said his name from far away.

"Yes, Lydia. Come on, focus. Open your eyes and look at me." He cradled her in his arms and crouched with her on the landing.

Realizing they were exposed if the stalker was still around, he lifted her and struggled to open the building door with his encumbered hands.

"Dammit!" he swore and kicked the door wide when he finally managed to turn the knob.

His cursing seemed to rouse her because she spoke. "What are you doing? Put me down! I don't want to make a scene."

He glanced around, but no one stood in the building's lobby. The search hadn't taken him long. Her office was in a converted Victorian house, like many buildings in Rolling Brook, thanks to the town's active historical preservation society, which continued to save more structures than developers could demolish. He knew because his mom ran the society.

What had been the entryway and parlor of the building were now a tiny lobby that serviced the offices it held. Apart from Lydia's practice, there was a dentist on the first floor and a graphic design studio in the basement, according to the sign by the staircase.

Looking down at her, he noticed her eyes had cleared. He set her on her feet but held on in case she collapsed again.

"I've got to go back out there and get the gift, and I need to sweep the area. Are you all right here?" He'd liked the feel of her in his arms, and part of him regretted releasing her.

Spotting a wingback chair by the door, he helped her into it. Whoever decorated this place had wanted to keep with the period for the décor. A marble-topped side table flanked it, and he set Lydia's bag on top.

"I'm going to call Sergeant Jameson and be right back. You're safe, okay?" He knelt in front of her and rubbed her hands.

At least she looks steady again. When she nodded, he said, "Good, I'll be right back." Giving her hands one last squeeze, he rose to his feet.

Outside, Dillon picked up the gift. This one was larger but wrapped in the same manner. He dialed Jameson on his cell as he scanned the parking lot for Owens.

Where is this bastard?

As he waited for Jameson to answer, he stared at the gas station across the street. Carter's had been there as long as he could remember, and it still looked the same.

The pumps had been updated out of necessity, but they

still sat open with no cover, while the little market looked like it hadn't been altered or even painted since the 1950s.

Old man Carter wasn't much into change, but he valued safety. That's why the metal butterfly roof was rusted, but a state-of-the-art security camera perched on each corner of the building. One of the cameras faced Lydia's building. Surely, that had seen something.

He growled in frustration, knowing he'd have to wait for Jameson to check it since he was suspended. "Come on, come on, man. Pick up your—"

"Jameson." His friend's clipped voice finally answered.

"It's Dillon."

"Hey, sorry. Was just meeting with the captain."

"And by meeting with, you mean getting yelled at." Dillon knew the captain's M.O. well.

"Yeah, the man is never happy. What's up?"

"I'm at Lydia Mason's office. There's been another gift. How soon can you get here?"

"I'm on my way."

"Thanks, James." Dillon disconnected and debated whether he should talk to the gas station clerk. Sighing, he resigned himself to the fact he'd get nowhere without his badge, and he didn't want to leave Lydia anyway. Thinking of her, he stepped back inside.

She wasn't where he'd left her.

He figured she'd gone up to her office, so he headed in that direction. Halfway up the stairs, another thought hit him, and he panicked. He should have swept the interior of the building before he'd left her alone.

What if the stalker had her?

Adrenaline surged, and he ran the rest of the way, his heart pounding in his chest. Her office door stood open this time as he stormed past Tanya's desk.

"Lieutenant!" The shocked receptionist tried, but he was already shutting the door in her face.

He turned to see Lydia standing and staring out the window next to her desk. Relief swamped him, and he tossed the gift on the couch.

Striding over to Lydia, he turned her to look at him. "Why didn't you stay downstairs? For a minute there, I thought . . ." Dillon stopped and stuffed away thoughts of his failure to protect her. "We have to talk to Jameson in a few minutes when he gets here."

Her face was expressionless as she explained, "I had to tell Tanya I was back. I didn't want her to worry."

"Did you tell her about the gift?" He searched her eyes for some form of emotion, but they remained impassive.

She shook her head. "Not yet."

Confused by her stoicism, he cupped her face and stared into those blank eyes. "Are you all right?"

Her sea-mist eyes darted toward the couch. "It's real, isn't it? That's the second gift?"

Caressing her temples with his thumbs, he answered, "Yes."

"Then he's coming after me again." Resignation colored her quiet response.

"No!" He told her sharply. "I'm not going to let him do that, Lydia." His voice strangled as he warned, "I can't lose you too. I won't—"

Dillon crushed his mouth to hers and kissed her with

all the anger and frustration he felt towards her stalker and his inability to find the man.

She kissed him back just as fiercely, and he was glad to have elicited an emotion from her, even if it was anger. Though, the longer he kissed her, the gentler he became. His hands shifted from holding her captive to caressing her. He moved them into her hair and loosened it from the French twist she'd styled it into.

Her head fell back as if the weight of her long locks had pulled it. He took advantage of her exposed neck and kissed his way down it. She moaned and sent a shot of heat straight to his groin. He contemplated laying her down on her desk when Jameson interrupted them.

"Hey, Tanya said—" Jameson stopped halfway through the door.

Lydia practically jumped away from him, and he couldn't blame her at that moment.

He turned his attention to Jameson and tried not to be angry at his friend when it was his own fault for pissing off the receptionist. "Jameson," he ground out through gritted teeth.

His friend cleared his throat. "Ah, I'm sorry. I didn't mean to barge in on you. Tanya said it was okay. Do you want me to wait outside?"

Before Dillon could tell him yes, Lydia spoke. "Of course not, Officer. Please come in."

Despite the flush gracing her cheeks, she moved to sit behind her desk as though everything was normal.

He shifted uncomfortably and gestured at Jameson. "Dr. Mason, this is Sergeant Jameson. He's taken over your case since my suspension."

She nodded as the sergeant greeted her.

Dillon hovered by the window while Jameson took a seat on the couch.

He nearly sat on the gift before Dillon pointed it out. "That's the second one."

"Okay," Jameson started. "Tell me about finding it."

He looked at Lydia, and she shook her head at him. Taking that to mean she didn't want to go first, he told Jameson they'd both been late for his session and found it at the doorstep.

She corroborated his telling and added the part about her nearly fainting, which he'd intentionally left out.

He'd figured that was her call if she wanted to relay it, and he was surprised she had. He knew it bothered her, but after getting caught kissing him, maybe it hardly mattered.

Jameson looked up from his notes, and his face was almost as red as his hair. "I think I know what happened after that."

Dillon laughed at his friend's embarrassment. "Yeah." He glanced at Lydia, and her mouth pressed into a thin line. Apparently, she didn't think that was as funny as he did.

"Did either of you notice anyone watching you when you found the gift? Or did you see anyone loitering nearby?" Jameson pulled his attention back to the stalker.

Lydia shook her head. "I didn't."

"James, the gas station across the street has surveillance. Can you see if they caught anything?"

"Absolutely. Good catch, Redland." With a nod, he stood. "I'll head over there now and check it out, then call you about what I find." Jameson grabbed the gift off the couch. "In the meantime, Dr. Mason, I recommend making a list of these events. By tracking his behavior, you'll have something to show in court if you need it."

She nodded. "Yes, I know. Thank you." Her voice was expressionless again, and he wondered what she was thinking.

Before Jameson left, Dillon grabbed his hand and forearm in a brotherly embrace. "Thanks, James."

His friend nodded in understanding. Dillon knew Jameson was taking this seriously despite the captain's lack of interest. He didn't have to worry about being kept up to speed.

After the sergeant left, Dillon hovered by the door, watching Lydia. He'd have liked to pick up where they left off, but he didn't think that was going to happen since she was staring past him as though lost in her thoughts.

He walked to her desk and waved a hand in front of her face when she didn't acknowledge him. "Lydia?"

She seemed startled as she looked up at him. "Yes?"

"I don't want you to stay alone tonight," he told her softly.

Her eyes flared at him. "You're still my client, Lieutenant."

He scratched at his chin. "Yeah, I figured you'd say that." He sighed. "It doesn't have to be me, but I don't want you left alone." His hands clenched into fists at the mere thought of it.

Her eyes looked tired as she answered him, "I don't know who to ask. Tanya has kids. She can't just drop everything and come over."

"I know you said your family wasn't close, but—"

"No. My father's in Greece. He moved back after my mother passed. Most of my family is there besides a few stray cousins in California."

He frowned at her news until he had an idea. "What about my sister, Daisy? Would you be okay with her spending the night?"

She looked surprised at his offer. "I don't think I even knew you had a sister. She lives here in Rolling Brook?"

Yes, she's my twin." Dillon shrugged. "She's single with no kids, so I'm sure she could stay over a few nights."

Lydia stared at him for a long moment as though she was "shrinking" his head, and he tried not to squirm under her gaze. He was relieved when she finally answered him.

"All right."

"I'll give her a call. Be back in a minute." He'd much rather have been the one spending the night at Lydia's, but at least with Daisy there, she wouldn't be alone. And it'd be easier to keep tabs on her through his sister.

* * * *

Lydia

Lydia was glad to have a moment to herself. Her thoughts scurried around in her head like frightened bunnies, and she was having trouble catching them. She tried to focus on the one that scared her the least—Dillon and how he'd kissed her.

Gently touching her fingers to her lips, she rose to look at herself in the mirror. She'd thought her mouth would have been swollen or bruised with a kiss like that, but there it was—a little on the full side like usual.

He'd been angry with her, though she wasn't clear on why. What had he said? Something like . . . *'I can't lose you, too.'*

That was interesting. She tapped her finger on her lip as she thought about his words. Did they have to do with losing Officer Spence?

She vowed to bring it up at their next session. Provided Samuel hadn't chained her up in a basement by then. An ice-cold shiver slithered down her back, and she pulled her thoughts back to Dillon.

She could've asked him about what he'd said tonight. But no. Now, she'd be spending the evening with his sister because she was too afraid to let him stay with her. How had she not known the man had a twin?

Lydia frowned. Probably because he barely opened up about anything, and since his sister wasn't involved in the shooting incident, he probably hadn't felt the need to mention it.

With a sigh, she sat back at her desk. What was she going to do about Dillon? He was still her client. No matter how much she wanted to let him in her bed, she had to resist.

But, oh, she so didn't want to sleep alone tonight. Not with Samuel coming after her.

It was unfair to want Dillon there to protect her when

he might have other reasons for wanting to stay. Still, she couldn't stomach the idea of facing Samuel alone when he came for her again.

Images of the last time he tried to abduct her flashed in her mind, and her hands began to shake. Her eyes stared at nothing as the terror she'd experienced then flooded her body.

"Hey, Daisy said she can do it." Dillon walked into her office and paused when she didn't respond. "Are you all right, Lydia?" He walked to her desk and leaned down to look into her face.

She didn't move a muscle. The moment when Samuel had tried to grab her was playing over and over in her mind.

"Lydia." He moved around the desk and crouched by her chair, turning it to face him.

She blinked when he shook her. "Stop that."

"Where were you?" he asked softly.

She gulped. "I was back in the parking garage . . . with Samuel." As she told him, her hands started to shake again.

"That's it. I'm taking you home."

"You can't. I have appointments." Her protest was half-hearted; she'd have trouble focusing on other people's issues in her current state.

"Well, tell Tanya to cancel 'em." When he pulled her to her feet, she nodded, too spent to argue with him.

CHAPTER 7

Lydia

Lydia yawned as Dillon pulled up in front of her house. Finding the second gift had left her emotionally drained and exhausted.

She turned to thank him, but he was already rounding the hood of the SUV. Feeling spent, she waited while he opened her door. Then, she let him help her out of the car. Although she was no longer shaking, she didn't mind his coddling. No one had cared enough to fuss over her in a long time.

"Thanks for seeing me home."

They reached the top of her steps, and she was scrounging through her large work tote for her keys when Dillon asked her, "Lydia, where's your camera?"

"Hm?" Distracted, it took her a moment to understand which camera he meant. "Oh." She stopped searching for her keys and met his gaze. "I have it, but . . . the security company's coming next week to install it."

His blue eyes fired at that. "It's not doing you any good in a box. Where is it? I'll do it myself."

She hesitated, but she was too tired to argue with him. "Fine." Shrugging, she went back to looking for her keys.

She was wondering if she'd forgotten them on her desk when, finally, her hand closed over them. Pulling them from the bottom of her bag, she unlocked the front door.

He stopped her from entering with a hand on her arm.

"What now?" she asked him, exasperated.

"Let me go in first. Stay right behind me when I do. I'm going to check all the windows and the back door."

"But—"

"Lydia . . ." he started through clenched teeth.

"It's just that I made sure they were all locked before I left this morning. How could he possibly have gotten in?"

"Maybe he didn't, or maybe he broke a window or jimmied a lock. I want to make sure either way." He practically growled at her.

"Right." Considering that possibility, she had to swallow past the lump in her throat. "Okay, go ahead."

She followed Dillon as he methodically searched her house. It was silly, but she was grateful she'd cleaned up after herself that morning. Not that she didn't usually keep it tidy, but some days were better than others on that count. First impressions were important, though; she didn't want his sister to think she was a slob.

He moved quickly through the rooms, and it didn't take him long to search them all. Her little bungalow was only around 1200 square feet. It had just enough space for her, with three bedrooms. One she'd turned into a guestroom and the other into an office-gym combo, though, admittedly, she rarely used it.

Thankfully, there was a second bathroom his sister could use. It was clean, as she'd yet to have a guest in her new house. She wondered what Daisy would be like.

"All clear." Dillon's announcement interrupted the picture she was trying to imagine of his sister.

He turned around abruptly and nearly collided with her; she'd been following right behind him like he'd asked.

He reached out to steady her or himself—Lydia wasn't sure—but his hands lingered on her arms. She looked up and her breath caught at the desire shining in his dark eyes.

Afraid of one or both of them losing control, she whispered, "Sorry."

He kept staring at her mouth. "You know, you smell like coffee and flowers."

Before she could think of how to answer, she realized he was going to kiss her. He leaned down, and she closed her eyes, knowing she should stop him, but she really didn't want to.

He surprised her when he sniffed at her neck instead, and her eyes flew open. "What are you doing?"

"Coffee and flowers—gardenia maybe," he told her with a grin.

"Thank you, I guess?" When she swatted at his arm, he released her.

Still smiling at her, he asked, "So where's this camera?"

Furious—though she would be hard-pressed to say whether at herself or him—she turned on her heel and headed for the storage closet where she'd stowed the security camera.

She'd just handed it to Dillon when someone knocked on her door.

"Helloooo?" a voice called.

"That's Daisy." Dillon started for the front door, and Lydia followed.

This was it. Time to meet Dillon's sister. She took a deep breath and followed him to the door, hoping how flustered the man made her wouldn't be apparent to his twin.

* * * *

Lydia

Lydia already knew Daisy. Well, she'd seen her at Shug's, the local diner where Daisy worked as a server. Of course, Lydia hadn't known the tall, raven-haired server was Dillon's sister. She did know she liked her, though.

Daisy's smile was open and friendly, and she'd hugged Lydia right away, unabashed by her brother's request to stay the night at a strange woman's house. They were going through the guestroom and bath when she heard cursing coming from outside.

"Does he know what he's doing?" she asked Daisy.

"Oh, sure, but it wouldn't be worth the hassle if he couldn't curse at it." She shrugged and grinned. "Men."

"Maybe we should check on him, just in case." Lydia worried about the potential damage he might inflict on her historic brick exterior.

Daisy followed as she made her way back to the front of

the house. As they reached the door, a police cruiser pulled into the driveway.

"Who's that?" Daisy asked.

Lydia walked down the steps and shielded her eyes from the setting sun. "Oh, it's Officer Jameson. I bet he has news about the gas station's surveillance cameras."

She turned to get Dillon's attention since he seemed absorbed in muttering over the wires hanging out of the side of her house. Thankfully, he'd drilled through the soffit, not her brick. "Dillon, Jameson is here."

He glanced over at her. "What?"

She pointed as Jameson climbed out of his cruiser, and Dillon followed her finger. "Oh, okay." He stepped down from the ladder he'd been hanging off of, and all three walked down to meet the sergeant.

"Redland, Dr. Mason," Jameson started. "Oh, Daisy. Uh, hi, I . . . didn't know you'd be here."

Daisy raised an eyebrow at him, but before she had a chance to answer, Dillon broke in.

"Yeah, I asked her to stay so Lydia wouldn't be alone."

"Oh, I thought you would've . . ." Jameson wisely trailed off at his friend's subtle headshake.

Lydia glared while his sister snorted.

Jameson cleared his throat and tried again. "That's good then, but I've got bad news, I'm afraid."

"Nothing on the cameras?" Dillon asked.

Lydia sighed. She needed to hear something other than bad news regarding Samuel.

"Not exactly. The camera captured the gift being delivered, but it looks like some young teenager. Didn't match Owens's description. I've got a printout, but it's pretty fuzzy." Jameson held out the grainy photo of a skinny teen standing in front of her building with the dreaded gift.

She shook her head at it. "I don't recognize him."

Dillon grabbed the photo for a closer look, and Daisy peered around his arm at it.

"So, he's trying to be smart this time around. He knows he's not violating the order if we can't prove he delivered them." The frustration was evident in Dillon's voice.

"But if he hired a courier, wouldn't that be proof enough?" Daisy piped up, and hope swelled in Lydia's chest. When everyone turned to stare at her, the woman shrugged. "What? I watch a lot of crime shows."

"Only if we could trace it." Dillon scratched at his five o'clock shadow.

The sound sent a bolt of heat through her body as she imagined that scruff tracing over her skin, and she had to force her gaze away.

Jameson nodded. "There'd have to be a paper trail. I can look into it, but he likely avoided that if he's smart enough to avoid the cameras."

The hope that had ballooned in her chest deflated at the sergeant's statement, and she sighed heavily. It was hard not to feel helpless. Jameson had been right—this was terrible news.

"So, what do I do?"

Dillon must have sensed her mood because he grabbed her hands and squeezed. "You don't go anywhere alone." His eyes were fierce when she stared into them. "Look,

Lydia, I know this is hard, but we will keep you safe. This camera"—he pointed backward with his head, and a sliver of warmth filled her chest over the fact he'd been willing to install it for her so she wouldn't have to wait another week—"and the one I'm going to put at the back door will help do that. Your neighbors have Owens's description, and they know to report it if they see him in the vicinity. I don't care how smart he thinks he is; he'll make a mistake, and when he does, we'll catch him."

She nodded but suddenly had the urge to giggle at the sense of absurdity she felt. Her life was turning into some suspense-heavy TV show. She could almost hear the music.

Wow, she was losing it . . . or she was just very tired.

Or both. Lydia sighed. Dillon still held her hands, and her gaze traveled back to his face. He looked so confident, so sure she was going to be safe.

If only he could stay . . . then I know I'd be safe.

She was still staring at Dillon, and everyone had gone silent. Was it obvious she was having a breakdown?

She glanced at Jameson and Daisy and noticed they were both looking at her. Had she missed something? She hadn't . . . said that out loud, had she?

Lydia cringed. It's not like Jameson and Daisy didn't think Dillon had already slept with her. She wondered if it was worth keeping him at a distance if that was everyone's assumption.

Thankfully, Daisy saved her from having to ask that question. "So, we should probably let Dillon get back to installing the camera, or he'll be doing it in the dark."

At Daisy's pronouncement, he finally dropped her hands. She tried not to miss the comfort they'd given her.

"Right." She turned to the sergeant and watched Dillon walk away out of the corner of her eye. "Thank you, Officer Jameson. Please let me know if you find anything on the courier."

"I will, Dr. Mason." He waved at Dillon, who had already climbed back up the ladder. "Daisy—"

Lydia would swear the man blushed.

"It was nice to see you."

Daisy smiled in response. "You too, James."

Yes, he's definitely blushing.

Lydia smiled to herself as Officer Jameson walked away. Something was going on between him and Daisy, and she wondered if Dillon knew.

Thinking of her grumpy lieutenant, she glanced over and watched his back stiffen as though he knew she was staring.

Always so guarded.

Sighing with exhaustion now, she tapped Daisy on the shoulder—the woman had been staring after the cruiser—and they headed back inside.

She was too tired to unpack the thoughts of Dillon that jumbled around in her head. That was a project for another day.

* * * *

Samuel

Samuel paced inside his hotel suite; his tall, lanky frame

and dark hair reflected in the glass of the windows. The Chicago skyline stretched out before him. He usually enjoyed watching the city at night.

The lights on the buildings seemed to float in the sky like fireflies. They typically calmed him down, but not tonight.

Tonight, his dark eyes flashed. He was in a rage over the fact that the cop had taken Lydia's gift—again.

This one had been an olive branch. He'd needed her to know he'd forgiven her for not accepting the first gift, but now the cop had stolen the second one before she could even understand that.

Why is he always there?

Samuel fumed at his thoughts of the policeman. He would give Lydia one more chance, and if she didn't accept this last gift, he'd have to find another way to get through to her.

She *would* understand. If he could get her alone, he'd *make* her understand.

His hands clenched into fists at the thought of what he might have to do to her. He didn't want to hurt her. But, if she wouldn't see reason . . . drastic measures were necessary, that's all.

It's not that he *wanted* to harm her, but that he would *have* to—for her own good. He was only trying to protect her from all the crazies out there. Surely, she'd understand that.

CHAPTER 8

Lydia

Lydia woke up the next morning feeling refreshed. The emotional strain from the day before had sent her body into self-preserve mode, and she'd slept more soundly than she had in weeks.

Yawning, she stretched and climbed out of bed. She felt so good she wanted to have a cup of coffee on her back porch and enjoy the sunrise. Pulling on her robe, she nodded along with her thoughts. She'd have her coffee, then call her father.

It was time he knew Samuel was back. She hated that the news would worry him, but he needed to know. Her father had nearly moved back to Chicago after what happened with Samuel last year; it had taken a lot of convincing to keep him from doing that.

Not that she wouldn't love to have her father closer, but he was happier in Greece with their family. Thinking of how he'd become a shell of his former self after her mother died,

Lydia knew he needed to stay in Greece.

When she stepped into the kitchen, she nearly collided with Daisy. "Oh!" She'd forgotten the other woman spent the night in her guestroom.

"I'm sorry!" Daisy said at the same time. "I didn't mean to scare you. I'm an early riser." She smiled. "I brewed coffee. Here, let me get you a cup."

Lydia found herself bemused. The woman moved around her immaculately updated kitchen as though it was her own; Daisy knew right where the coffee mugs were stored.

When she opened the mahogany cabinet that held them and handed Lydia a steaming cup of the delicious-smelling brew, she decided she didn't mind. "Thank you."

"I was just about to take a cup out back. You have a beautiful spot there," Daisy told her.

She tried not to be annoyed that she'd now have to share her morning plan. "Yes, I was thinking of doing the same thing."

"Oh well, I don't want to intrude—"

"You wouldn't be. Join me," Lydia responded automatically out of politeness.

"I love your house." Daisy gestured when they'd reached the back porch and sat on a vintage cast iron loveseat.

Glass-topped end tables flanked it. The furniture was placed against the back wall of the house, leaving the view out over the rolling, tree-covered hills open for her to enjoy.

Like the couches in her living room, Lydia inherited the patio furniture with the sale of the house. The cushions on the loveseat were a bright orange and yellow floral pattern, which had to be from the 1960s. They perfectly matched the sunrises she loved watching from them.

"I've been living in apartments for years, but this makes me think about moving."

Lydia smiled at that. "Thanks. I know what you mean. I always lived in apartments in Chicago. It was so nice to get away from that and have my own space."

"I'm sure." Daisy smiled brightly at her, and she was struck by how similar the woman's eyes were to Dillon's. They were the same deep blue, and she found it disconcerting enough to glance away.

She trained her eyes on the sunrise instead. "It can get really quiet here, though."

Bright colors started to paint the sky. It did feel nice to have company. Maybe she'd been living alone for too long, but after the drama with Samuel, she'd retreated from people, afraid to open up in case they'd judge her.

"Oh, yeah. I know that's an adjustment moving from the city."

"Yes, especially since I'd always had roommates and, later, a boyfriend living with me."

"Had? So, you're not with anyone now?"

Lydia raised an eyebrow at Daisy's prying but didn't mind answering. "No, the last man I was seeing left me over the stalker thing. He thought I encouraged it." She frowned as she remembered how Brice had accused her of doing something to warrant the gifts from Samuel.

Daisy shook her head. "Ugh, what a jerk. Men can be so dense."

"Mm," she hummed in agreement.

Daisy glanced sidelong at her. "Speaking of men who are dense, my brother's not seeing anyone . . ."

She had to laugh at Daisy's not-so-subtle hint. "Your brother is my client."

The woman frowned at that, making Lydia wonder why it upset her.

"Is he okay? These past few months, he hasn't been himself. Jake and I were worried but if he's seeing you, then at least he's getting help." Daisy paused and stared down at her coffee mug. "The thing at the farm . . . it messed him up inside. He wouldn't talk about it with me, but I could tell."

Leaning over, she squeezed Daisy's arm in reassurance. "He's working through it, but these things can take time."

His sister looked up at her with tears in her eyes. "Thank you for helping him."

"Of course. It's my job."

Daisy's stare lingered. "Is it? Just a job, I mean. With Dillon?"

Frowning at her question, Lydia didn't want to answer. She didn't have to, but she liked Daisy despite—or maybe because of—her directness.

"Truthfully? I'm attracted to him, but as much as I'd like to take that somewhere, I can't. Not while I'm counseling him. It would be unprofessional."

"Uh-huh," Daisy trilled. "There are worse things than being unprofessional—in my opinion." She grinned. "I'd hate for you guys to miss out on something because you're worried about what people will think."

"Mm-hmm," Lydia murmured. She didn't have an

argument for that. In fact, she was trying hard to disagree with it.

* * * *

Dillon

Dillon grumbled at his reflection in the mirror. He'd been dragged to the local tailor shop and decked out in a suit. The last time he'd had one on was at Spence's funeral.

He caught himself as he instinctively reached up to rub at his chest. At least this suit was blue. His brother—or, more likely, his future sister-in-law—had chosen navy suits with light yellow shirts for the wedding party.

"It looks fine." He was tired of the tailor preening over him.

Of course, his brother, Jake, disagreed. "Stop whining, Dillon. The legs are still too long, and you know it."

"Well, how long does it take to mark a pair of pants?" He looked pointedly at the elderly tailor, who harrumphed and bent his balding head back down to continue measuring and chalking.

"What's got you so impatient, brother?" Jake crossed his arms and stared at Dillon's reflection in the full-length mirror.

"It's nothing." He looked away from Jake's probing gaze.

"Hot date?" His brother teased, gray eyes lighting with mirth. "Going out with, what was her name? Sylvia?"

He glared at his older brother. "No. You know I broke things off with her."

His relationship with Sylvia had ended shortly after the

shooting. He'd pulled away, not just from Sylvia but his family too, Dillon admitted.

Sylvia hadn't stopped him, though; honestly, he hadn't wanted her to. It had been easier to throw himself into work than deal with what he'd been feeling.

So, maybe he'd yet to have a serious—take home to meet the parents' kind of relationship—but he was only thirty-two. Besides, his job was more important; at least it had been until he'd gotten suspended.

"So not Sylvia, then," Jake kept teasing. "Maybe this new doctor you're seeing? Lydia, is it?"

"It's not like that with her, and you know it." He wished his brother would stop prying. Ever since Jake had found Blair, his interest in Dillon's love life had intensified. It was like he thought his happiness with a fiancé meant everyone else needed one.

Not that Dillon didn't want one—eventually—but he had other things to worry about right now.

"That's not what I heard . . ." Jake's face split with a shit-eating grin.

He ignored the grin. "Daisy doesn't know what she's talking about."

"Who said I heard it from Daisy?"

"What? Who then?" Lydia wouldn't be happy if someone were spreading rumors about his relationship with her.

"This is a small town, Dill. You know people talk—"

"What are they saying?" he practically yelled at his brother.

"Hey, calm down. I'm only teasing." Jake raised his arms in surrender. "It was Daisy. She told me she was staying with Lydia. I know you've been going for counseling, and I'm glad, brother."

He'd clenched his fists and had to make a conscious effort to relax them. The poor tailor stared at him like he'd lost his mind. Maybe he had. At least, he thought he was getting close.

"Sorry, Jake."

"You like her then?" His brother asked him softly as though afraid Dillon would snap at him again.

When had he become the kind of person people had to handle with care?

"Yes, I like her," he could admit it. "But she wants to keep things on a professional level. I'm trying to respect that."

When Lydia looked at him yesterday like he was the only thing she wanted, he'd nearly given in—despite Jameson and Daisy standing right there. But he'd known she wasn't thinking clearly, not after the way she'd reacted when she'd realized Samuel was coming after her again.

He hadn't wanted her to do something she'd regret. But, man, it had been hard to walk away.

Her scent drove him crazy. Whatever floral perfume she wore was intoxicating. It smelled like gardenias—heady and sweet.

His mom was really into flowers when he was growing up. She'd made him and his brother learn which ones were which so they'd know the right blooms to pick when she sent them to the garden.

He'd never forgotten the scent of her gardenias. They'd been his favorite back then, and they were becoming his favorite now for a whole different reason.

Jake was nodding at him. "I get that, but if you want something more . . . maybe you should try and change her mind."

A grin slowly spread across Dillon's face at his brother's words. It matched the one Jake wore. The grins would've pegged them as brothers if the resemblance hadn't been clear in their dark hair and tan skin.

"Maybe I should." He hadn't felt this light in days. Thoughts of convincing Lydia to agree to more than a professional relationship distracted him enough that he no longer minded that he was wearing a suit and being poked and prodded.

"If you succeed, she could be your date to the wedding." Jake winked at him in the mirror, and Dillon wanted to roll his eyes.

My brother, the matchmaker.

CHAPTER 9

Dillon

The late afternoon sun shone in the window behind Lydia's desk. It reflected off the light-colored wall and created a spotlight around her.

As if Dillon needed another reason to look at her.

Even when he wasn't in her office for a counseling session, the doctor was all he could think about. Before today, it had been two days since he'd last seen her, but the thought Jake had planted in his head about convincing her to take their relationship beyond the professional level had kept her at the forefront of his mind.

Though he sat across from her now, he had trouble focusing on what she was saying. Inevitably, his eyes would be drawn to her lips as she tapped her pen against them.

She had such a fascinating mouth. Her bottom lip was overly full and should have made her look like she was perpetually wearing a pout, but instead, that too-full lip made her look sexy as hell, especially when she chewed on it like she was doing now.

Lydia cleared her throat, and he drew his gaze up to her eyes. The look on her face made it clear she was aware of where his mind had gone.

Her obvious discomfort made him smile. He needed her to stop fighting the attraction and just give in. "What was that, Doc?"

"I said, I think we should have Officer Spence's family join us for your next session."

That wiped the smile from his face. "What? Why?"

He hadn't seen the Spence family since the funeral, and he didn't think they'd want to be reminded of what they'd lost.

"You've told me you blame yourself for Officer Spence's death. Don't you want to know how his family feels about it?"

Defeated, he let out a heavy sigh. "Maybe they blame me too."

"Do you honestly think that?"

He felt like he deserved their blame, but before he could answer her, there was a knock at the door.

She kept his gaze as if to say he hadn't gotten off the hook yet while she called out, "Come in."

Jameson opened the door and stepped inside. "Hey, Dr. Mason." He noticed Dillon on the couch. "Oh good, Redland, you're here too."

"What have you got for us?" He sat up straighter, hoping it was a lead.

"More questions than answers, I'm afraid."

He heard Lydia's sigh at Jameson's response. She was as frustrated as he was that they hadn't found anything on Owens yet.

"Unfortunately, Owens didn't leave a paper trail when he hired that kid as a courier. We dusted the gift for prints. Owens's weren't on it, but the kid's were. I ran them through the system but didn't get any hits."

"Yeah, that was a long shot. We've seen he's smarter than that," Dillon grumbled as he rubbed the back of his neck.

Jameson looked at Lydia. "Do you know why he would gift you Veuve Clicquot and a Hermes scarf?"

Her eyes widened at the mention of the gifts, and Dillon wondered what she knew about them.

"If there's anything you can tell us, it might give us a lead," his friend prompted.

She slumped down in her chair, frowning. "I don't see how the story behind the gifts will help you find him."

He rose, unable to stand her looking so defeated. Moving to her desk, he curled a finger under her chin and lifted her gaze to his. "Hey, whatever it is, Owens coming after you is *not* your fault. But if you tell us, there's a chance it could provide something else to look into."

She grimaced and shook his hand off. He tried not to be annoyed that she was pushing away the comfort he'd offered.

"Fine. The champagne is likely a reminder of when we shared a bottle. Samuel had just stood up to his parents, which was a breakthrough in his therapy. He'd brought the champagne with him when he came to tell me about it. It had been the end of the day, and he'd wanted to crack the bottle open to celebrate. I was happy for him, and I didn't want to cause him to regress by turning down the offer, so" she paused, disgust filling her voice when she admitted, "I drank it with him."

"Okay." He wanted to hold her but didn't think she would let him. Reining in the desire, he backed up and spoke to Jameson. "So maybe we look into Owens's parents? What if he's staying with them?"

"Oh." Lydia looked surprised as if she hadn't considered that.

Jameson nodded. "What can you tell us about them, Dr. Mason?"

"Their relationship is strained. It was one of the things that led to Samuel seeking counseling. His family is wealthy. Regular Chicago socialites. Their names are Denis and Miranda Owens—"

Jameson cut her off with a whistle. "As in Owens Wellness? The medical technology company?"

"Yes. Apparently, you've heard of them." Both men nodded. "Well, they threatened to disown Samuel if he didn't go to counseling, and that's when he found me."

"Why did his family want him to go to counseling so bad?" He figured Owens had to have done something pretty severe for them to threaten to cut him off.

"I don't know the exact circumstances. He never opened up to me about it, but I do know it was related to his inability to control his anger."

Dillon winced as she shot him a glare. She had to be remembering the day they'd met when he'd lost control, and his anger had been directed at her.

"And the scarf?" he probed gently, hating seeing her upset, but they needed any information she might have to help them catch this creep.

Lydia looked puzzled. "I don't know, other than he offered to buy me one once. I brushed it off, but that's when I knew things had gone too far, and I needed to end his sessions."

"Okay, well, we can contact his parents. Find out if they know any places he frequents or where he might be staying," Jameson hedged as he wrote in his notebook.

"Thanks, James. Let us know what you find." He nodded at his friend as he showed him to the door.

After Jameson left, Dillon started to walk to Lydia, but she pointed at the couch. "We're not done with your session, Lieutenant."

So, I'm Lieutenant again.

Dillon sighed and sat down when what he wanted to do was gather Lydia in his arms and kiss her until she forgot all about Owens.

"The Spence family. Do I have your permission to contact them and ask them to come in during your next session?"

"Yeah. It's not like the whole town doesn't already know I'm in therapy." He scowled.

She was probably right about talking to the Spences, even if he dreaded what they might say. He owed them that much.

* * * *

Lydia

As the door closed behind Dillon, Lydia let out a tortured sound and dropped her head in her hands. She'd made so many mistakes with Samuel, and now they were coming out.

Perhaps Brice had been right, and she *had* encouraged the gifts by allowing things to go on for as long as they had. Samuel's behavior rang warning bells from the start, but she'd thought she could handle it. She was a professional. Her job was to help people like him, and she'd been so confident she could that she'd put her profession *and* her life at risk.

And now Dillon . . . the way he'd treated her. Lydia choked back a sob. She didn't deserve his comfort, but she would help him find his own.

She knew she was pushing him away; she'd already had to navigate them out of uncomfortable territory after she'd asked him what he'd meant by his 'can't lose you too' comment.

It was clear to her that he felt he'd failed by not saving Officer Spence, and now he was projecting that fear of failure onto her situation. All she needed was to be another reason he couldn't move past Officer Spence's death. If that happened, she'd probably need to find a new profession.

Taking a deep breath, she instructed herself to stop wallowing in self-pity and focus on what she *could* do to start earning retribution for her past lapses in judgment. She picked up the phone to confirm Dillon's next session with Officer Spence's parents.

He'd been right—everyone did seem to know his business. The Spences had actually approached her, requesting to join one of his counseling sessions. They'd been appalled to find out he'd cast blame on himself, though she wasn't sure how they'd known he had. They must have a contact at the county who let that information from her report slip.

She shook her head. She didn't know how to stop those kinds of leaks in a small town. But since they'd contacted her, she was on board. Dillon needed to hear the Spences didn't hold him responsible for their son's death. She hoped it would finally help him let go of the guilt he harbored before it ate away too much of the man he used to be.

CHAPTER 10

Dillon

Even though three days had passed, Dillon's next session came too quickly. He was nervous and avoiding eye contact with the Spences, knowing he couldn't handle the resentment surely on their faces.

They sat on the couch in Lydia's office, and he perched halfway between them and Lydia's desk in a chair she'd pulled from somewhere.

Of course, now she had a chair. He gripped the arms and tried not to think about the fact he was alive and the Spences' son was not. Stomach roiling at the thought, he swallowed to erase the sour taste lingering in his mouth.

"You didn't fire those shots into my boy, Lieutenant. And the man that did will spend the rest of his days behind bars. It's not fair. But it is justice. That's what gets us through."

At Mr. Spence's words, his head snapped up, and he

locked gazes with the man. His light blue eyes were kind, and they held no rebuke like Dillon had expected them to.

As he continued to stare, he noticed how much Nathan had resembled his father. Mr. Spence had the same blonde hair and rangy build.

Still stunned, he glanced at Mrs. Spence when she addressed him, "He looked up to you, you know that? You saw his potential and took him under your wing. All Nathan wanted was to follow in your footsteps, Lieutenant. Don't let him down by beating yourself up this way. He died a hero . . . don't take that from him."

Her last statement ended with a sob, and he woke from the shock their words had caused.

Walking to her side, he crouched and clasped her hands. "I'm sorry, Mrs. Spence. You're right. Nathan deserves better." He drew in a ragged breath. "He is a hero, and that's how I'll remember him."

Dillon glanced at Lydia as she placed a hand on Mrs. Spence's shoulder and offered the woman a box of tissues. The Doc had been so quiet he'd almost forgotten she was there.

She spoke quietly, "Thank you for coming in today, Mr. and Mrs. Spence. Opening up to one another about Nathan is cathartic and honors his memory."

The Spences nodded and rose to leave. He was at a loss for words when Mrs. Spence hugged him fiercely. As her short, plump frame enveloped him, the tension he'd been holding onto for months drained away.

When she released him, Mr. Spence clasped him on the shoulder. "Thank you for everything you did for our boy.

You're a good cop, Lieutenant."

Tears pricked Dillon's eyes; he blinked and swallowed hard to clear them. "Thank you." He didn't know how else to respond. Emotions swirled in his gut, and he wasn't sure if he was going to be sick or woozy.

Thankfully, the Spences didn't expect more from him as Lydia showed them to the door.

He practically collapsed on the couch and stared at nothing when Lydia interrupted his jumbled thoughts.

"How are you feeling?"

He was dazed enough not to be guarded. "I'm not sure, honestly. How . . . how can they be so forgiving? How are they not angry?" He looked at Lydia in wonder.

"It's easier to let go of those things when guilt isn't hounding you. You understand they don't blame you for Officer Spence's death?"

Dillon wasn't sure that fact had fully sunk in yet. "Yeah, I just . . . how?" His eyes pleaded with her to help him understand.

"Blame won't bring their son back. You didn't fail him, Dillon. The Spence's never thought that. They know Nathan's death isn't fair, but you gave them justice by capturing the man who took his life."

He slowly nodded as what she said stopped the storm in his gut. "Justice."

"Yes." She reached out and squeezed his hands. "You gave them that. Now, can you honor their wishes and let your guilt go?"

He felt a flutter in his chest when he looked into her eyes. Something that had been holding onto him for too long loosened its hold. "I will. I owe it to Spence."

A new resolve settled over him. He'd been so focused on blaming himself for Spence's death that he'd neglected to honor the man and his sacrifice.

But no more.

Spence deserved better. He deserved to be remembered as the hero he was. So that's what he'd do. He'd stop focusing on his own guilt because that was selfish. By holding himself responsible and believing he'd failed, he'd potentially damaged his career—a career Nathan Spence had dreamt of having.

Dillon internally winced as he thought of the poor example he'd been setting and how Spence would've been disappointed in him.

"Good." Lydia nodded.

She still held his hands, and watching her reaction, he brought them to his lips.

He smiled at her sharp intake of breath as he placed a gentle kiss on the tops of their joined hands. "Thank you."

Her lips parted, and her tongue darted out to lick her bottom lip. He held her hands and waited. The next move was hers. His muscles tensed in anticipation when her eyes glossed over, and she leaned toward him. Finally, Lydia was going to kiss *him.*

He tried not to groan as his craving for her flooded his body. Battling the urge to close the distance between them, he did groan when a knock sounded on the door, causing Lydia to blink abruptly and back away from him.

"Dr. Mason, your next appointment is here."

He growled at the receptionist's voice.

So close.

"Thank you, Tanya. I'll be right out," Lydia responded.

"I guess that's my cue to go," he muttered as he rose, but he wasn't ready to leave. "Lydia—"

"You should go, Lieutenant. My next client is here." She walked back to her desk and made a show of finding her pen and notepad.

He sighed. So, she wanted to avoid having a conversation about the fact she almost kissed him.

"Thanks again, Doc." He opened the door when she only nodded and wouldn't meet his gaze.

Knowing she was busy, he let her off the hook for now, but they were going to have that kiss . . . and a lot more.

Grinning at the thought, he saluted Tanya and practically floated out of Lydia's office.

CHAPTER 11

Lydia

Lydia heard the pounding on her front door, and her heart leaped into her throat.

What if it's Samuel?

She swallowed and tamped down her fear, peeking out the window to see who had decided to pay her a visit after eight p.m.

Noticing the red SUV Dillon drove, since having to relinquish his police cruiser, Lydia relaxed until she realized he would be angry with her because Daisy wasn't there. Wincing over that, she opened the door for him.

"What the hell, Lydia? Why didn't you call me when Daisy couldn't stay? I only found out she had to pick up an extra shift because I went to Shug's for dinner."

"Nice to see you too, Dillon." She *was* genuinely glad to see him. She already felt safer with him at her door, but she couldn't help noticing the way his wet t-shirt clung to his chest. And that was a problem.

"Are you going to invite me in? Or do I have to spend the night out here?"

She dragged her eyes back to his face and gulped, unsure she could handle Dillon sleeping under her roof. "Um, well, I—"

He snarled at her through clenched teeth, "In case you weren't aware, it's raining. I got drenched. The least you could do is offer me a towel."

"You're right. I'm sorry." She opened the door wider and stepped back to let him in, then shut it and locked it behind him.

He was creating a small puddle on her floor. "Don't move. I'll be right back with some towels."

"Thank you." He shook the rain from his head while she searched for a towel.

She was on autopilot as she headed down the hallway toward the guest bathroom. Opening the small linen closet just outside the room, she mindlessly grabbed towels. Her thoughts kept circling back to Dillon and what he'd looked like with his wet t-shirt molded to his chest.

He'd been angry with her, but she'd still been turned on.

Lydia shook her head at herself. She'd never been so attracted to a man before. He clouded her thoughts and made her want things she shouldn't.

Sighing because he would want to stay since Daisy couldn't, Lydia wondered if she should let him. His sister was a much easier roommate. She enjoyed her company, and they'd quickly become friends.

But Dillon . . . she wanted him to stay out of her fear of

Samuel, but letting a client sleep under her roof, even if she did manage to keep her hands off him, was totally unprofessional.

He stood shirtless in her entryway when she returned. She had to take a deep breath to calm the heartbeat that wanted to race at the sight of his deeply tanned torso. He wasn't beefy, but the muscles of his arms, chest, and—she swallowed as her gaze dipped lower—abs were all well-defined.

He was holding his wet shirt in his hands and must've wanted to wring it out but thought better of it.

Smiling at that, she handed him a towel. "Thanks for not wringing that out on my hardwood floor."

He returned her smile. "Yeah, it's pretty soaked."

She reached for his shirt. "Here, let me. I'll take it to the sink."

Relief flooded her when he handed the shirt over, and she could turn away from his bare chest. Walking to the kitchen, she released the breath she hadn't been aware she was holding.

She was in trouble.

As she wrung his shirt out over the farmhouse-style sink, she racked her brain for a scenario where he stayed and they didn't end up in bed together.

Distracted by her thoughts, she jumped when Dillon came up behind her. He was close enough that she could feel his warm breath on her neck, and she shivered.

"I think it's as good as it's going to get," he said as he reached around her for his t-shirt.

She was frozen in place as his body molded around

hers. His masculine scent, accented with the freshness of rain, invaded her nose and muddled her thoughts.

When he pulled his shirt from her hands, it dripped cold water droplets on her arm, clearing her brain.

"Wait!" She grabbed his shirt and turned around, using it as a shield to keep him from coming any closer. "It's still wet. I'll put it in the dryer." She looked down at his jeans as she said this, wondering if they were wet enough to also warrant a spin in the dryer. "Are your pants . . .?"

He was quiet, and she swallowed when her eyes met his. They were hot, and she knew what he was thinking. She started to edge away from him, toward the laundry room, to give them some much-needed distance.

He stopped her retreat with a hand on her arm. "Why didn't you call me?" His gaze was equal parts anger and need.

"I was going to, but I . . . I knew you'd want to stay."

"Would that be so bad?" he whispered. "Earlier, you were going to kiss me."

"No, I—"

"Are you a liar now, Lydia?" His eyes dared her to try and explain away that almost kiss.

She sighed. He was right—she would have kissed him if they hadn't been interrupted. There was no point in lying about it.

"You can stay. On the couch."

"Are you sure that's what you want?" He ran his hand up her arm and caressed her cheek.

He was staring at her mouth, and all she could think was, "No." No, that wasn't what she wanted.

She wanted him to take her—to make the choice for her, so she wouldn't blame herself for being unprofessional.

His presence made her feel safe, and she desperately needed that.

But he's still my client.

Though they'd had a breakthrough today, there was more for him to work through, wasn't there? Her brain was starting to fog over again as she stared into the deep blue wells of his eyes.

He cocked an eyebrow at her, and she realized she was supposed to be answering his question.

"Yes. I'm sure." Her voice sounded strained to her own ears, and she knew she hadn't convinced him.

"My pants are okay."

"What?"

He grinned at her confused expression. "They're not that wet. I'll lay them out to dry when I sleep."

"Oh." Her thoughts instantly went to him sleeping without his pants.

"Sooo, where *am* I going to sleep?"

"The couch. Er, no. You can use the guestroom since Daisy's not here. It's this way."

Still gripping his wet shirt, she rolled her eyes at herself. If she had any hope of them making it through the evening without jumping each other, she needed to get a grip on her libido.

* * * *

Lydia

Lydia woke, gasping for breath from a nightmare that had been all too real. Shaking, she tried to block out the feeling of having been paralyzed by fear.

In her nightmare, Samuel had succeeded in locking her in the trunk of his car, and she'd been unable to scream for help, much less fight back.

She needed a drink after that.

Thirsty and wide awake now, she headed for the kitchen. As she drew near, she heard Dillon's voice. He was talking to someone on her back porch.

Confused that someone else would be in her home at close to midnight, she padded softly down the hall to see what was going on. Her bare feet made silent steps on the hardwood floors.

"—are you sure, James?" She heard him asking as she reached the back door.

Oh, he's on the phone.

She stepped out onto the porch and chased away a shiver as her feet touched the mosaic terracotta tile floor. It had cooled considerably without the sun to warm it.

The moonlight slanted across Dillon's face, highlighting the strain on his features. The soft illumination also alerted her to the fact he was dressed only in boxers. She swallowed.

Even with the dim lighting, she could make out his well-muscled form, and her pulse jumped. The hint of rain still permeated the air, and it reminded her of the way he'd smelled when he'd leaned around her at the kitchen sink.

Too tempting. Way too tempting.

He heard her approach because he spun around; a look

of relief crossed his face when he saw it was her. "Okay. Yeah, I'll tell her. Thanks, James."

He ended the call and stared at her. His gaze raked over her silk pajama set, and suddenly, she was aware of how thin the material was.

Barely resisting the urge to cover herself, she asked him, "What was that about?"

He avoided her question. "Sorry, did I wake you?"

She thought about retreating back into the house when he stepped toward her. The look in his eyes was making her anything but calm.

"No, I, I had a nightmare." She shivered as she recalled the reason she'd woken in the first place.

At her shiver, Dillon closed the distance between them and rubbed her arms. "Want to talk about it?"

She slightly shook her head as she stared into Dillon's eyes. His hands on her had caused all thoughts of her nightmare to fade away.

How can his eyes be so blue?

Even in the moonlight, they gleamed like sapphires. They were hard like the gem but not cold.

Her pulse raced at the way he looked at her.

No, not cold at all.

Reaching up, she placed her hand on his cheek. It was deliciously warm, and his stubble prickled her palm. She was wondering how that scruff would feel on certain other parts of her body when he sighed and closed his eyes.

"Lydia." Her name was almost a prayer as it escaped his lips.

Knowing she'd crossed into dangerous territory, she

dropped her hand and stepped back. Her brain cleared without those bright blue eyes holding her captive, and she remembered his phone call.

"What did Jameson have to say?"

The way his expression fell, it certainly wasn't good. "He talked to Owens's parents. At first, they weren't very cooperative, but when he told them their son was stalking you . . . some information came to light."

She recognized his stalling. Whatever that information was, she didn't think she'd like it. "And? What is it, Dillon?"

"They told him why they'd wanted Samuel to go to counseling in the first place."

She looked at him expectantly, but he didn't continue. "Just tell me, please. The more you draw it out, the more worried it's making me."

His chest moved as he took a deep breath. "He nearly killed his girlfriend." At her sharp intake of breath, he quietly added, "he strangled her with a Hermes scarf. The housekeeper saw the struggle, and when she threatened to call the police, Owens stopped. The family paid for the girlfriend's medical care and added a hefty sum for her silence."

She felt her eyes grow wide as her hand flew to her mouth on a gasp. How could she not have known? She'd treated Samuel for almost a year!

All that time, she'd never suspected he was capable of this—to nearly kill someone! Even when he'd tried to abduct her, she'd thought him unstable but not *homicidal.* How had she not seen? To strangle some poor woman with a scarf . . .

The scarf!

As realization dawned that he'd meant the same thing for her, her body started to tremble. She could feel her breath hitching, and her legs turned to jelly. Wobbling, she made it to the outdoor loveseat and collapsed. "The scarf, Dillon. He gave me a scarf."

He rushed to her side. "He's not going to get to you, Lydia. We won't let him. You're safe, and you need to calm down."

He rubbed her back, but it did precious little to stop the panic from stealing her breath. "I can't breathe," she gasped.

Dillon grabbed her face and turned it to look at him. "You're hyperventilating. You have to slow your breathing. Listen to me. You're safe, okay? Take a deep breath."

Her panic slowly subsided, staring into those sapphire eyes again, and she focused on doing as he'd asked.

"That's good, Lydia. Another. Now exhale. Good girl." He kissed her forehead gently. "Just like that. Slow, deep breaths. In." His lips whispered over her cheeks. "And out."

Her heart rate accelerated again, but it wasn't panic that caused it this time. Dillon's lips were mere inches from hers.

If she was going to die, she might as well enjoy the time she had left.

He was still holding her face, so she grasped his wrists and used them to pull his mouth to hers.

At the contact, she hummed in approval. This was what she wanted, unprofessional or not.

CHAPTER 12

Dillon

Lydia had finally kissed him. Though Dillon's body stirred at her touch, his brain nagged him that she was vulnerable and he was taking advantage.

When she traced his lips with her tongue, he told himself to pull away, to slow things down, but his hands had other ideas.

Before he'd realized what he was doing, he'd cupped her breasts and held them, measuring their weight. She moaned, and the sound was intoxicating. For weeks, he'd imagined what she'd feel like in his palms.

Lydia's mouth grew more insistent, and he feared he'd passed the point where he'd be able to stop. The only thing he could think of now was having more of her. Craving it, he let her in, and when her tongue swept over his, his blood rushed south.

Her hands traveled up his back, found his shoulders, and clung when he shifted her onto his lap. Her scent mixed with the smell of the flowers in the pot beside the door. Heady and sweet, it hung in the warm night air, inciting his hunger for her. When he pressed her center onto the bulge in his shorts, she gasped, breaking the kiss.

"God, I want you." He leaned back against the floral cushions of the loveseat, away from that tempting mouth, offering her the chance to change her mind but hoping like hell she wouldn't take it.

"I want you too." The sea green of her eyes had darkened with her desire.

His pulse jumped at her words; that was all the confirmation he needed, and he wasted no time getting her exactly where he wanted her.

He flipped her onto her back and captured her mouth again. The cast iron loveseat made a scraping sound as it slid against the tiles with their movement.

Her legs came up to straddle him, and he growled, nipping that lush bottom lip of hers. When he released her mouth, he caught sight of her nipples. They stood erect and visible through the silk pajama top she wore.

Wanting to make her as crazed as he was, he brushed his thumbs against them. Her head fell back, and with the long line of her neck exposed, he lavished his attention on it, kissing and sucking his way down that beautiful column.

Sighing, she arched her chest toward him in invitation. He answered by closing his mouth around those full breasts, one then the other, through the thin fabric she wore. Tasting, pleasuring, he feasted on Lydia.

She clawed at his back as he pushed her close to the

peak, and the scratching sent a dark thrill through him. Starving for her flesh now, he peeled off her pajamas.

"You're so damn sexy," he growled. Lydia had curves for days.

Cuffing her hands above her head, he sampled every inch of her, his roughened cheeks scraping her smooth skin and leaving a trail of red in their wake.

Her breath caught when his mouth traced the inside of her thighs. "Dillon."

His name was a plea, and he was eager to give in. Testing her, he explored her heat with his tongue. The sound she made in response had the blood roaring through his veins.

Freeing her hands, he focused his attention there. She was as wet as he'd been when he'd gotten caught in the rain. Once she started to writhe against him, he pushed her over the peak.

She cried out his name and he watched that gorgeous body shudder with her orgasm.

More, she's more than I imagined.

Before she could go limp, he took her mouth again and began rekindling her arousal with his fingers, determined to make her as desperate as he was.

"I need you," she panted as her hands and lips raced over him, clawing and biting until she was wrestling him out of his boxer shorts.

He groaned in pleasure when her hand closed around him. As she teased him, he found her breasts again with his mouth and drove her to the edge.

When her skin had flushed, and her heart pounded as

hard as his own, he grabbed her hips. "I've wanted to do this for weeks."

"Do it, then." Her voice was a demand, punctuated by the sharp staccato of her breaths.

He thrust inside her and lost all control.

Finally. It was all he could think.

Her body bowed toward him, and the feel of her drove him wild enough that his fingers dug into her hot flesh as he pounded into her. She felt like ecstasy, and he was helpless to do anything else.

Never enough.

He'd never get enough of her. The harsh sound of their labored breathing and the slap of their bodies together resounded in the stillness and broke the quiet of the late hour. His pace was frenetic, but she matched him; their frenzied rhythm drove all thoughts except those of pleasure from his mind.

His breath hissed out in wonder, and he didn't think Lydia could be more beautiful than she was when the moonlight lit her face, shining on her like some Grecian goddess as her eyes closed, her muscles contracting around him. The pleasure was too much. He grunted as he watched her, then followed with his own release.

The strength left his arms, and he collapsed on top of her. She'd staggered him. His heart hammered in his chest, but he wasn't sure it was merely from the exertion. That had been incredible. *She* was incredible. Who would have thought Dr. Mason had such passion?

A satisfied smile lit his face, but as she remained still, he worried she regretted what they'd done. He hoped that wasn't the case because he already wanted to do it again.

Propping himself up on his elbows, he stared down at her. Her eyes were shut, and her hair was a dark halo around her head. "Lydia?"

She grinned with her eyes still closed. "Hmm?"

He took the grin as a good sign, but he had to be sure. "Are you all right? I didn't hurt you?"

She opened her eyes and stretched, catlike. The movement pushed her body into his, causing his appetite for her to spike again.

"Better than all right," she answered with a sleepy smile.

She looked so satisfied he kissed her on the nose. "Good, because we're going to do that again." He climbed off her and lifted her to her feet.

She chuckled and glanced around the porch. "I don't think I'll be able to have coffee out here again without remembering."

He grinned down at her. "Oh, you'll think of me. But not just out here."

He wanted her to think of him as often as she consumed his thoughts, which was all the damned time. Dillon felt a flutter around his heart.

Ignoring it, he lifted her into his arms. "Where's your bedroom, Doc?"

She linked her hands behind his neck with a smile. "I'll show you."

He carried her into the house for round two. With his initial need satisfied, this time, he was planning on going slow and savoring every delicious inch of her.

CHAPTER 13

Samuel

The carefully wrapped package crumpled in Samuel's hands as the cop answered Lydia's door without a shirt.

He didn't recognize the older man visiting her house this early in the morning, but he didn't care.

His pulse pounded in his ears, and his face twisted into a mask of rage as betrayal sliced through his gut.

So, she'd let the cop spend the night.

She'd have to be punished for that. And the cop, well, the cop would pay for it, too.

Thinking of the ways he'd make that happen, Samuel's pulse calmed, and he released his grip on the package.

Looking down at it, he sighed. He'd hoped things would go differently, but now that wasn't possible. Smoothing the wrinkled blue wrapping paper, he placed the gift in the passenger seat.

Perhaps, if she learned her lesson, he'd give it to her, but first, he would make her see how wrong her actions had been. She belonged with him and him alone. It was time she accepted that.

* * * *

Dillon

Dillon leaned against the kitchen counter, the granite cold against the bare skin of his back, as he sipped his coffee and waited for the interrogation that was bound to come from the man seated at the kitchen table across from him.

Lydia's dad watched him and let the silence stretch, expecting it to make Dillon uncomfortable.

As a police officer, he knew how it worked. He'd been caught off guard by the man's arrival at seven a.m., but now, with the caffeine waking him up, he wasn't about to give in.

He'd already tried the friendly approach when he'd answered the door. That had been shut down before he could even get out a "Nice to meet you, sir," so he'd wait, and they'd see which one of them broke first.

After nearly five minutes, her dad cleared his throat, and Dillon tried not to smile—he'd won that round.

"So, how you met my daughter?" The sound of his native tongue accented the words.

He wasn't ready to reveal his personal issue, so he simply told him, "I'm a police officer. We've worked together."

"Humph. Police. Is dangerous work." His dissatisfaction with Dillon's profession was evident.

Yeah, his job could be dangerous, but he recognized

that her dad wouldn't like any profession he named, judging by the way the man glared at him. Maybe he should go wake Lydia.

"What I call you?"

"Dillon, sir."

Her dad nodded and pointed at his chest. "Nikolaos."

He felt like this was a trap. Were they going to get through introductions this time? If he reached his hand out, would it be slapped away?

He studied Nikolaos's face. The Mediterranean sun had darkened his olive skin and etched lines around his eyes. His forehead was wrinkled, but Dillon wasn't sure if that wasn't from the frown still aimed in his direction.

Her dad was probably in his early to mid-sixties, and you wouldn't know it apart from the lines on his face. He was in remarkably good shape with dark eyes and hair the same color as Lydia's, though his had streaks of gray in it.

He was about to risk it and hold out his hand when Lydia waltzed into the kitchen. She was headed straight for him and hadn't noticed her father yet.

Thankfully, she was wearing a robe and not the barely-there pajamas she'd had on last night. There was a wicked gleam in her eye that he would've liked to explore had they been alone.

Instead, he stood abruptly and gestured to the kitchen table. "You have company."

Surprised, she whirled and gasped, "Baba!"

Nikolaos stood and moved to hug Lydia, who'd frozen in place in the middle of the kitchen.

"What are you doing here?" she demanded when she'd

gotten over the shock.

Nikolaos glanced at him before responding, and Dillon wondered what that worried look meant.

He was left wondering because Nikolaos's answer was given in Greek. Dillon stood silently by while they conversed in a language he didn't understand. He sipped his coffee and watched as Nikolaos's hand movements became more animated, and their voices climbed in volume.

At one point, Nikolaos spit the word *kamaki* in his direction, and she answered with a stream of words he didn't need to understand the meaning of to know their intent. She was defending him, and it made him smile. The arguing continued while Dillon refilled his coffee, but then Lydia had apparently had enough.

"We're being rude, Baba." Her voice was edged with frustration, but she handled it well. Turning to him, she offered an apology, "I'm sorry, Dillon. It's easier for my father to speak Greek."

He nodded at them, but later, he would ask her what *kamaki* meant. "That's all right. I understand."

The smile she gave him in return was tentative at best. Whatever her father had said was troubling her.

"Baba, help yourself to some coffee. I need to speak to Dillon alone for a minute." She grabbed his hand and pulled him to the back porch.

When they'd reached it, she turned around and shut the door, clearly not wanting to be overheard. He could tell she was agitated. It made him want to kiss her and soothe away her nerves.

Stepping toward her, he cupped her face, but before he could lean in, she jerked away from him.

Frowning at her quick retreat, he asked, "What's wrong?"

She let out a heavy sigh and avoided his eyes. "Last night was a mistake."

Brows furrowed at her words; he fought the urge to rub a hand over his heart. It felt like she'd sliced him there with that one horrible statement. Last night hadn't been a mistake, and there was no way he would let her off that easily.

"That's bullshit, Lydia. And you know it." He masked his hurt with anger.

She flinched, but he didn't back down.

"You weren't thinking it was a mistake a few minutes ago when you were ready to jump me again in your kitchen." He stepped toward her and lowered his voice. "What did he say to you?"

There were tears in her eyes when she finally looked at him. "It's not that. Or not just that," she amended. "He's worried about Samuel being back. It's why he came. But Dillon, you're still my client. We shouldn't be . . ." She waved her hand between them. "I can't. It's unprofessional. I can't let the lines cross again. Look what happened with Samuel and—"

He cut her off with a roar. "You'd compare me to him? For fuck's sake, Lydia! I'm not a stalker! I'm trying to keep you safe from him!"

He paced away from her, running a jerky hand over his face as he tried to regain control.

Her eyes widened at his harsh words. "I'm sorry. I didn't mean it like that. I know what we have is not the same as what happened with Samuel. But I still think we need to take a step back for now."

He felt a painful tightness in his throat as she pushed him away. Trying for a smile, it came out more as a grimace. "All right, Doc. If that's what you want."

She nodded.

"But you're wrong if you think last night was a mistake."

"Dillon—"

"You won't be alone? Your dad will stay with you?" He cut her off again, unwilling to listen to her offer another justification against what they'd shared.

"Yes. He'll stay with me for the week."

He nodded briefly, then left as she stared after him. He had to get away from her before he said something he'd regret.

How did—yeah, he'd admit it—the best night of his life turn into the worst morning of it?

Shaking his head in disbelief and without stopping to tell her dad goodbye, Dillon bypassed the kitchen, grabbed the rest of his clothes from the guest bedroom, and left, not even bothering to put them back on.

CHAPTER 14

Lydia

Lydia watched Dillon for his reaction as she announced, "From what I've seen from you today, I feel you're ready to go back to work."

She paused, his lack of reaction surprising her. They were back in her office. Initially, she had been worried that he might not show up for his session after the way they'd parted. But he had.

Nearly a week had passed, and she struggled daily not to think about the night they spent together. She'd been relieved they'd been able to have a professional session today. After talking to him for the past hour about the critical incident, she'd come to the conclusion that he'd finally moved past it.

He was no longer having the recurring dreams about Officer Spence's death. There'd even been no signs of continued guilt or anger over the incident.

Not once had he reached up to rub his chest when

they'd talked about Officer Spence. It appeared to her that he'd resolved his feelings over the shooting.

So why doesn't he seem pleased that he can get back to being a cop?

Had what she said not sunk in? "I'll make my statement to the county for your reinstatement."

He only nodded at her, his expression unreadable. "Thank you, Doc."

She frowned. "Is something wrong?"

His response was puzzling. She'd thought her announcement would have made him ecstatic, but at this point, she'd settle for a smile or *something* to show that he was happy about her agreeing to let him get back on the job.

"Are we done with the session?"

She glanced at her watch. They'd gone over his hour by five minutes already. "Yes. And though I'm considering your required counseling sessions concluded, I hope you know you are welcome to schedule one any time you feel the need."

She wished they were closer so that she could reach for his hand and give it a squeeze, but it was probably for the best that he was seated several feet away from her on the couch.

Until he was officially cleared by the county and back on the police force, she wasn't ready to continue any type of personal relationship with him.

He stared at her with an intense look in his eyes. She wasn't sure how to decipher it, but her phone rang before she had the chance to. "Yes, Tanya?"

"Lydia, the hospital's on the other line. They said it's urgent." Tanya's usually clear voice quivered, and Lydia's stomach tightened.

"All right. Put them through."

Dillon stood but hesitated as if he wasn't sure if he should give her privacy or not.

She waved him back down and heard the other line connect. "Hello, this is Lydia Mason."

"Hi, Ms. Mason. This is Nancy with Dale County General. There was a man admitted earlier." She heard the sound of shuffling papers. "His name is Nikolaos." The woman struggled to pronounce the unfamiliar name. "Nikolaos Pallas. You were listed as his emergency contact."

"What's happened to my father? Is he all right?" Her voice rose several octaves, and she clenched the phone so hard her fingers turned white.

Dillon came and crouched next to her desk, placing a hand on her shoulder while she waited for the hospital's response.

"Well," the woman said hesitantly, "we're not sure."

"What do you mean?" Lydia was trying desperately to understand how that could be the case.

"He's been moved to the burn unit—"

She gasped.

"—for now. He was brought in late this morning after a Good Samaritan saw him collapse on the street. He was feverish and confused. We had him under observation, during which time a rash formed on his skin. It's since advanced to blisters. The doctors are running tests now.

I'm sorry for the troubling news, Ms. Mason, but we need you to come in and complete his paperwork."

Lydia was numbly nodding when Dillon squeezed her shoulder. "Yes, of course."

"Thank you. If there are any medications you know your father was taking, please bring a list of those with you."

"I will."

"Do you need directions to the facility?"

"No. I know where it is."

"We'll hope to see you shortly, then."

"Thank you."

The hospital disconnected, and she sat frozen until the beeping on the line startled her into action. She sprang to her feet, launching Dillon's hand from her shoulder.

"I have to get to the hospital."

He stood as she searched for her keys.

"What happened?"

"My father's been admitted. They don't know what's wrong with him. I have to . . ." She closed her eyes and worked hard to swallow the tears that threatened.

"I'll go with you." He placed his hands on her shoulders, and she opened her eyes.

There was no reason for him to go with her—not if they were only therapist and client. But the concern in his gaze and her response to it told her that wasn't really the case. Maybe it had never been. She needed him.

Overwhelmed, she nodded. "I can't find my keys."

"I'll drive you." He grabbed her purse off the floor, took her hand, and led her out of the office.

Tanya's eyes were wide when Lydia and Dillon stepped

through the door holding hands, but she didn't care. The only thing that mattered to her at that moment was getting to her father. Let the town talk about her relationship with Dillon; she had more important things to worry about.

"My father's in the hospital. I have to go to him. Please cancel my appointments for the rest of the day."

"Of course! Lydia, I hope he's all right."

"Thank you, Tanya."

When a look of true sympathy crossed the receptionist's face, Lydia turned away before she lost the tight control she had over her emotions. "Let's go, Dillon."

* * * *

Lydia

Lydia blinked, and they were at the hospital. The loop of her thoughts had so consumed her that she couldn't remember the ride over.

Dale County General Hospital loomed in front of them. It was an austere six-story building built in the Brutalist style, and it looked brutal to her. The roughened concrete that made up the exterior did little to communicate anything other than the sense of staring at a giant tomb, as though when one stepped inside it, they'd never walk back out.

Tears pricked at her eyes, and she furiously blinked them away. That wasn't going to happen to Baba.

Dillon reached over and squeezed her hand as she sat lost in thought. She wanted desperately to see her father, but at the same time, she was afraid to. Ever since her mother's death, hospitals had filled her with a sense of dread.

Six years ago, she and Baba had sat for hours waiting for news of her mother inside the operating room. She'd been simply walking across the street in Chicago when a distracted driver hit her. The internal bleeding had been too extensive, and her mother hadn't made it.

"Lydia?"

She turned to see her staring at her with worried eyes.

"I'm okay; it's just . . ." She glanced back at the daunting building. "My mother died in the hospital, and now"—her voice hitched with unshed tears—"my father's in the ICU."

He tugged on her arm until she faced him. "I'm with you, okay? We'll do this together."

Relieved that he would be by her side, she nodded and gathered her courage. "Okay."

* * * *

Dillon

Nikolaos's condition was a mystery to the doctors and nurses at Dale County General. When he'd been admitted, they'd thought he was dehydrated and suffering from a severe case of the flu, but his symptoms had quickly gotten worse.

At first, the rash on his skin suggested an allergic reaction, so they'd begun running tests. Before the results had even come back, however, the rash had turned into blisters that spread to his mouth, eyes, and nose.

Without any readily discernible cause for them, the

doctors rushed her dad to the burn unit. That's where Dillon and Lydia were currently waiting.

They'd already donned and shed the yellow gowns, blue gloves, and masks required when visiting inside a patient's room. Lydia had wanted to stay with her father, but the nurse in charge of changing the dressings covering his blisters had kicked them out to the waiting room.

It was empty apart from them. He glanced over at her, and she was staring at one of the drab green chairs as though it held the answer to her father's condition.

Nikolaos was heavily sedated to ease the pain from the blisters that had begun traversing his skin. Still, Dillon knew Lydia desperately wanted to ask her dad what happened.

He squeezed her hand as they sat and waited, not knowing what to do except be there for her.

"Whatever it is, he's getting the best possible care right now."

She nodded, but her gaze didn't stray from the chair.

He wanted to distract her and pull her thoughts from wherever they held her. "What does *kamaki* mean?"

She blinked and turned to look at him. "What?"

Her expression showed confusion, but at least she focused on him instead of the chair.

"What's *kamaki*? Your dad called me that the morning he found us together." Dillon's lungs constricted; it still hurt that she'd pushed him away. Concentrating, he managed to pull in a breath. "I've been wondering about it ever since."

She blinked again, and a strangled sound escaped her

lips. "It means . . . womanizer, is probably the easiest way to translate it."

He smirked. "Womanizer, huh? So that's what your dad thinks of me." It almost made him laugh. He figured her dad's opinion was warranted considering the situation in which they'd met, but if that's what Lydia thought of him . . . Suddenly the term didn't seem so funny.

"You don't think that, do you? Because I'm not. You know that, right?"

Okay, yeah, he'd never had a serious, long-term relationship, but that didn't mean he used women. He was raised better than that.

The relationships he'd been in had been exclusive—if brief. There just hadn't been one he couldn't see himself living without until *her*.

After a heavy pause, she answered, "I don't know, Dillon. I don't really know you. During our sessions, you barely opened up to me. And that was all related to the incident. Maybe you are a womanizer." She shoved to her feet and started pacing between the rows of chairs in front of him.

He had a sinking feeling in his gut. "Is that why you pushed me away?" he asked Lydia softly.

She didn't acknowledge his question as she continued to pace. "You realize we've never even been on a date? We slept together, and we . . . we weren't even . . ." She grasped her hair in her hands as she struggled for words. Finally, she stopped pacing and looked at him with a bewildered expression. "I've never done that before."

"I don't know what you want me to say to that, Lydia."

His hands clenched as the anger rose to cover the pain she so easily inflicted on him. "If you're implying that I seduced you into bed with me—that you weren't willing . . ."

He waited for her to say something—to tell him that wasn't what she meant. That she didn't think so little of him. But when several agonizing seconds passed in silence, he was forced to acknowledge that maybe she did.

He scrubbed his hands over his face in frustration. "I'm going to get us some coffee."

As he stalked away, he wondered what the hell he was doing. Why was he so caught up in a woman who didn't seem to give a shit about him?

He'd spent the better part of a week frustrated on multiple levels as he tried to give her the space she'd asked for. And things hadn't changed. She still didn't want him.

Fuming at that fact, he wanted to punch something. He mindlessly sought a vending machine when he admitted that wasn't the whole truth.

Lydia did care about him. Look how she'd helped him deal with Spence's death. He just hoped it was on more than a professional level.

CHAPTER 15

Lydia

Lydia stared after Dillon, knowing she'd hurt him. She hadn't meant to, had she?

If she was being honest with herself, she wasn't sure. She didn't think he'd tricked her into bed with him, but she'd meant it when she'd told him they barely knew each other.

Never had she slept with a man she'd known so little about, and it scared her. The way her body responded to Dillon, she ended up reacting without thinking things through first, and that wasn't her style—not usually.

Sighing over the words she couldn't take back, she turned to see if the nurse was finished redressing her father's wounds and froze in fear.

Samuel was standing right in front of her.

"Hello, Lydia." He grabbed her upper arm as he smiled at her.

She opened her mouth to scream, but no sound came

out.

"You don't want to do that. Not if you want me to help your father," he sneered at her.

She struggled to find her voice through the trembling that had taken over her lips. "What, what do you mean?"

"Oh, they'll figure out what's wrong with him eventually, but your father will suffer in the meantime. You know, it's good they put him in the burn unit." Samuel chuckled. "The disease will literally continue to burn his skin off. Doesn't that sound painful?"

He reached with his free hand to brush her hair behind her ear, and she flinched at his touch.

"Is that what you want to happen to your father? Or are you going to come with me and put an end to this?"

A surge of anger flooded her, and she tried in vain to jerk her arm free from his grasp. "What disease? What are you talking about?"

The way he grinned at her sent shivers down her spine.

"Stevens-Johnson syndrome. I'm afraid the drug I slipped into your father's coffee at the cafe causes quite a severe case of it, even in people not genetically predisposed to the disease. During clinical trials, the drug also had an accelerated reaction in participants aged fifty and older." He glanced toward Baba's room. "Seems to be affecting your father rather quickly because of that. As I mentioned, the burning of the skin is rather painful, but it's the sepsis that will kill him. One little infection, and he'll be in organ failure. That is unless you agree to come with me."

She knew the longer she stalled him, the better the chance of Dillon returning. "Where did you get that kind of drug, Samuel?"

He smirked at her. "What? You think I'm lying? My family runs a medical technology company, or don't you remember? They conduct trials on a lot of different drugs. Mom and Dad were particularly invested in this antipsychotic." His smirk turned into a petulant frown. "They wanted to use it on me. But then it caused all those people to die, and it never made it to the market." He shook his head. "Such a waste of money."

Her eyes widened at his callous response. "How many people died in the trial?"

He gave a slight shrug but still didn't release her arm. "A dozen or so."

Her face blanched in horrified disbelief. "That doesn't bother you?"

"Are you counseling me, Dr. Pallas?" He smirked at her, and it occurred to her that's what he wanted from her—what he needed to hear.

"It's Dr. Mason now. And yes, I am. We can start your sessions again, Samuel. But you have to help my father first. Tell me how to stop the Stevens-Johnson syndrome."

He was staring at her thoughtfully, but then he shook his head. "Let's take a little walk, shall we?"

As he dragged her toward the freight elevator, the fear took her over. She tried to scream again, but all she managed was a whimper when Samuel clamped a hand over her mouth and shoved her inside the elevator with him.

Where's Dillon?

It couldn't take that long to find coffee. She shouldn't

have hurt him. That was stupid.

Stupid, Lydia!

He was probably avoiding her now because of it, and she desperately needed him.

The elevator doors closed, and Samuel removed his hand from her mouth. The shiny metal walls reflected the deranged gleam in his dark eyes, and she stiffened as his hand moved to tighten around her waist.

"Are you going to come with me willingly? I won't give you your gift otherwise."

She closed her eyes on a shudder of disgust as his breath brushed her ear. The man was delusional, but playing along held a higher likelihood of keeping him calm.

"What gift would that be, Samuel?"

"Your father, of course. Don't fight me, and I'll tell his doctors they need to administer a cyclosporine. It'll suppress his immune response, so his body stops reacting to the antipsychotic with blisters and burning."

There was no way she trusted him to call her father's doctors. If only she could get away from him, she'd tell them herself.

She took a deep breath to try and ease the fear that wanted to leave her frozen again.

Think, Lydia!

There had to be a way out of this. The elevator doors pinged open onto a dimly lit hallway she guessed was in the hospital's basement. She sincerely hoped it wasn't the morgue.

Shivering involuntarily at the thought, she had to at least try and make a run for it. After taking another deep breath, she slammed her elbow backward and connected it with Samuel's stomach. The move surprised him enough to break his hold on her, so she ran.

Why had he brought her down here? There had to be an exit somewhere. Her thoughts raced, and her heart pounded in her chest as she passed one dark door after another. Nearing the end of the hallway, she spotted a stairwell leading up.

About to step on it, there was a sharp yank on her hair, and Samuel pulled her back against his chest. "Now, now, Lydia. I can't give you your gift if you try to run away."

She was gasping for breath as much from fear as the exertion. Pain radiated from where he still held her hair. "Please, Samuel, you don't want to do this."

"No, I don't." He eased the hand in her hair. "I don't want to hurt you, but if you run again, you leave me no choice." He released her and turned her back down the hallway toward the elevator.

She heard him sigh behind her.

"If you fight me, I'll be forced to hurt you. It'll be like Candy all over again. She didn't listen, so I had to—" He shook his head, and Lydia caught the movement out of the corner of her eye as it sent his dark hair flapping.

Another wave of fear swamped her when she digested his words. "Who was Candy?"

He sounded sad when he told her, "She was my best friend in high school. We were meant to be together, but she wouldn't see it. I tried, Dr. Pallas. I tried to convince her—showered her with gifts. But she didn't accept them. We were arguing, and she refused me. So, I had to strangle her."

The way he so dispassionately admitted to killing a woman had her pulse racing in trepidation.

"Of course, I had to make it look like a suicide. She was under a lot of pressure to win a scholarship and get into college. That could've been too much for anyone. No one questioned that she took her own life." He chuckled. "I used the Hermes scarf I gave her. It was almost poetic to have her hang herself with it."

She was back to trembling, unsure how her feet moved forward when she was shaking so much.

Samuel had not only attempted to murder a woman, but he'd succeeded in doing so years prior. The only thing Lydia could think about was that she would be number three.

She'd run in the wrong direction for an exit. They passed the elevator, and he pushed her through a set of double doors out into the startlingly bright late afternoon sun.

Squinting her eyes, she flinched when he began pulling her toward a vehicle.

Not again. She nearly fainted when another wave of fear battered her.

"Well, now. That's one way to go willingly."

His voice brought her back to her senses. No way was she passing out and winding up in that car.

She dug her nails into her palms and was about to try a scream again when the most wonderful thing she'd ever heard beat her to it.

* * * *

Dillon

"Stop right there, Owens." Dillon wished for his weapon as he carefully approached the stalker and Lydia. They were ten yards ahead of him, headed toward a black Audi SUV.

At the sound of his voice, Owens froze and jerked Lydia around with him. She appeared terrified but unharmed.

The bastard had his arm around her, though, and Dillon couldn't tell if he was holding a gun on her or not.

Fear for her safety wanted to intrude, but he pushed it away, knowing it would debilitate him if he let it in. His stomach had already become a solid rock of nerves when he returned to the waiting room and found her gone.

Now, his eyes were cold and sharp as he calculated the best way to get her away from Owens. "Lydia's not going anywhere with you. Let her go."

The stalker snarled at him and pulled a nine-millimeter pistol from behind his back.

Dammit!

Owens must have had the gun tucked in the waistband of his pants. There were hardly any vehicles in this part of the parking lot, which meant Dillon didn't have many options for cover. He hoped the department would get here fast.

He'd yelled for the nurse to call the police after she'd told him she saw Lydia get into the freight elevator with a man. Then he'd raced down the stairs looking for them. He'd figured if Owens had been the man with her, he'd want to get her out of the hospital, so he'd come out to check the parking lot.

Thank God he'd been right.

"You're wrong about that, cop. Lydia's coming with me, and you're going to die."

She whimpered, and Dillon inched closer. He had the passing thought that at least if he got shot, it was only a few steps to the O.R.

The way Owens held the gun on him made it clear the man had never used one. Hell, the nutcase might still have the safety on.

"No, you're going to jail. And she's staying with me."

Police sirens cut off Owens's reply, and Dillon used the distraction to his advantage. As the man glanced toward the road, he rushed forward. Before he reached the stalker, though, he turned back around and fired his gun.

Lydia's scream tore through the air.

Dillon felt a sting in his right side as he tackled Owens. She went down with them, but out of the corner of his eye, he saw her scramble up quickly. Thankful for that, he slammed Owens's hand on the asphalt, knocking the pistol free. Then he flipped him over and pinned him to the ground.

He held the stalker there as the police cruisers pulled into the hospital parking lot. "Like I said, Owens. You're going to jail."

Not happy with that scenario, the man growled and tried to buck Dillon off, who cursed the fact he didn't have his handcuffs when Jameson appeared.

"Redland," his friend's eyes were full of concern. "I'll take it from here."

Unfazed, Dillon hauled Owens up with him and handed the bastard over. "All yours, James."

Jameson nodded and cuffed Owens. He was watching Dillon closely as he called for a paramedic.

He looked sharply at his friend. He hadn't thought he'd hurt the bastard that bad when he'd tackled him.

"Dillon." At Lydia's voice, he glanced over at her, and her eyes were wide. She pointed at his chest. "He shot you."

He looked down at his right side and saw the copious amount of blood that had already stained the white of his favorite Cubs shirt.

"Oh." He was confused because he didn't feel anything. *Shouldn't a gunshot wound hurt?*

But as he continued to stare at the blood, his world exploded with pain, and he dropped to his knees. "Fuck, fuck, fuck!"

Lydia rushed to his side and tried to put pressure on the wound. As soon as she placed her hands over him, though, his side lit like it was on fire, and his breath hissed out.

"Sorry! Sorry!" Silent tears fell down her cheeks as she stared at him.

In the background, he heard Jameson yelling, "I said I need a paramedic, now! We've got a gunshot wound!"

"Oh, Dillon. I'm so sorry!" Her eyes were full of regret, but he wasn't going to let this be her goodbye. No matter what happened to him.

"Be my date to my brother's wedding next weekend?" His words were hard to push out through the teeth he'd clenched against the pain, but he managed.

"What?"

"I'm not dying today, Lydia, so stop looking at me like that." He was in too much pain to be dying. "I probably won't be up to dancing, which is a shame because I'd love to dance with you."

He attempted to reach up to touch her face with his right hand but thought better of it when it made the pain ten times worse. His eyes watered, and he had trouble seeing her face when she responded.

"You want to dance with me?"

He struggled to nod. "I want to have a relationship with you—dates and everything."

She was smiling through the tears when she told him, "I'd like that."

His face stretched into a modicum of his usual grin. Then, the paramedics lifted him onto a gurney. Lydia squeezed his left hand before it was pulled free when the orderlies rushed him inside.

She followed, and he focused on her for as long as he could, but soon, he was hooked up to an I.V. that made her face and the rest of the world fade away.

CHAPTER 16

Lydia

Watching the careful rise and fall of Dillon's chest, Lydia silently begged him to wake up. She'd been sitting by his side for the past hour since they'd wheeled him out of the operating room. His ordinarily bright complexion looked sallow against the stark white of the hospital sheets.

The constant beeping from the heart monitor rattled her nerves instead of settling them as she battled the fear that it would suddenly flatline, even if, logically, she knew that wasn't likely to happen. The doctors had assured her that Dillon was going to be fine.

The bullet hadn't penetrated anything vital; it passed through the flesh of his upper right torso, missing both his lung and his liver. He was—quite possibly—the luckiest victim of a gunshot wound to the chest that Dale County General had ever seen, or so the doctors had told her.

That was all good and well, but she needed to see it for herself. She needed to stare into Dillon's sapphire eyes and see his crooked grin spread across his face again.

So many things had been running through her mind while she'd waited by his side. Thinking about how she'd purposely tried to push him away made her cringe. Now that she'd had time to analyze it, she understood that she'd hurt him out of fear—fear of the feelings she'd developed.

She wanted—no needed—to apologize.

Holding his hand, she willed him to open his eyes. His doctors had said the anesthesia would wear off soon, but an hour didn't seem like 'soon' to Lydia. She debated whether to call the nurse when his hand twitched in hers.

"Dillon?"

He stirred and opened his eyes with a groan.

"Dillon!" She was so relieved she pounced on him.

"Ow! Lydia, damn, that hurts."

She pulled back immediately. "I'm sorry. I'm sorry. Oh, Dillon! I'm so glad you're okay!"

"I told you I wasn't going to die."

Inexplicably, she burst into tears.

What's wrong with me?

She'd never cried so much in her life, not even when her mother had passed away.

"I'm sorry. I'm just so relieved. I can't believe you did that—rushing a man with a gun!"

"What was I supposed to do? I couldn't let him take you." He reached for her hand and pulled her down to sit beside him on the bed while she tried to dry her tears.

"Thank you. You saved my life." Her response still came out a bit watery.

Bringing her hand to his lips, he kissed the back of her

palm. "How long was I out for?"

"A little over two hours."

The longest two hours of my life.

"So, what's my prognosis, Doc?"

She smiled for the first time in what felt like days. "Well, Lieutenant. You're the luckiest G.S.W. that Dale County has ever seen. The bullet made a clean exit and missed any vital organs, but you have some muscle damage that could take weeks to heal. My best guess? You'll be out of here tomorrow at the earliest."

He grinned at her and raised an eyebrow. "And how long until I can perform . . . other activities?"

She surprised herself with a bark of laughter. "Oh, I don't think you're allowed any strenuous activity for at least a week, but we'll have to verify that with your doctor."

"I can wait." He winked at her and pulled her in for a kiss.

She melted into his lips, enjoying that this man she'd come to care so much for was still alive. She could easily imagine the guilt she would have had to work through if he hadn't made it.

Sighing, she pulled back. "I'm sorry for what I said earlier. I don't really think you tricked me into bed with you."

He stared at her as though he wanted to say something but wasn't sure he should.

She lifted her palm to his cheek and let herself sink into the deep blue pools of his eyes. "I care about you—a lot. And I want to get to know you better."

The crooked grin she loved spread across his face.

"Good, because I care about you a lot too."

Warmth filled her heart, spilling out to shine on her face. "My father doesn't think you're a *kamaki* anymore. I told him what you did—how you saved me from Samuel."

Relief showed on his face. "He's okay then?"

She nodded and explained, "It was all Samuel. He drugged my father with some kind of antipsychotic. It was from a treatment trial that Owens Wellness conducted, but the company ended it because it was too dangerous. I don't know how Samuel got his hands on it, but he told me how to counteract the drug's effects when he took me. That was his plan—to offer to save my father if I went with him willingly." She shook her head at the absurdity of it and Dillon squeezed her hand.

"After they wheeled you away, I went to the burn unit and talked to Baba's doctors. They confirmed his blood tests had found an unknown drug in his system. I convinced them to talk to Owens Wellness, and thanks to Officer Jameson's help, who wanted me to tell you he needs your statement when you're feeling up to it."

Dillon only nodded at that; she supposed it was the cop in him who recognized it as necessary.

"They confirmed it was the drug from their clinical trials. Then, the doctors started my father on an immunosuppressant. He's doing better, but he'll still be in the hospital for a few days until the chance of an infection is gone."

"I'm glad he's going to be okay."

"Me too. I still can't believe how crazy this day has been." She paused, knowing she had to tell him. "Samuel told me he killed his high-school best friend. He strangled her and hanged her with a Hermes scarf to make it look like a suicide." Recounting it, she shivered.

His hand tightened around hers. "The bastard's going to pay, Lydia."

His eyes were fierce, but they didn't scare her. She felt the same need for justice. "Yes, he will."

"DILLON!"

She turned around at the shriek as Daisy launched herself into the room. A man and a woman Lydia hadn't met but would bet were her brother and his fiancé followed Daisy at a much more sedate pace.

His sister didn't stop at the bed but leaned down to hug him before Lydia could warn her not to.

"Ow, ow, Daisy! Be careful, I'm wounded."

She pulled back, and tears shone in her eyes. "You deserve it, you blockhead. First, Jake, now you get yourself shot. I'm going to have gray hair before I'm thirty-five at this rate."

"Hey, mine didn't land me in the hospital," Jake complained.

Thinking they'd like some time alone, Lydia stood and backed up so Dillon's family could be by his side.

Jake took her place and embraced his brother's left arm. "Glad you're all right."

A silent exchange of relief passed between them when Dillon squeezed Jake's hand, but then his face fell with worry. "You told Mom and Dad?"

"Yeah, they're on their way back from Mackinac now."

He winced. "They didn't have to cut their anniversary

trip short."

Dillon started to explain at Lydia's questioning look, but they all chimed in. As voices flew around her, she gathered that Brock and Sandy Redland had spent a week in Mackinac Island, Michigan, for as long as the siblings could remember. The couple went each August to celebrate their wedding anniversary ever since they'd honeymooned there forty years ago.

"You know how mom is. She'd never enjoy herself, knowing you were laid up in the hospital. Get ready for lots of lecturing and coddling." Jake smirked at his brother. "I had the same experience a few months ago when I got shot, and my wound was only a graze. You're in for a whole lot worse."

Watching their conversation, Lydia began to fidget with the sleeve of her blouse.

Huh, I lost a button at some point today.

The more they talked around her, the more awkward she began to feel. She was about to step out of the room when Daisy stopped her.

"Lydia, don't leave," his sister called her back to the bed. "Where are our manners?" She pointed at the two people in the room Lydia didn't officially know. "If you haven't figured it out yet"—she had—"this is my brother Jake and his fiancé Blair. Guys, this is Lydia."

Everyone turned to stare at her, and she suddenly felt self-conscious. Would they blame her for what happened to Dillon?

"Hi," she ventured.

Before she had more time to worry about it, Jake

hugged her, lifting her feet off the floor. Surprised, she laughed at his exuberance. "It's great to finally meet you, Lydia," he told her when he set her down.

Blair smiled behind him. The petite blonde had extraordinary green eyes. Lydia was happy they were friendly when the woman extended her hand. "Nice to meet you."

She shook her hand. "You, too."

Officer Jameson appeared at the door. "What is this, a party?" he joked.

At his entrance, everyone began talking at once, greeting Jameson and peppering him with questions. She wasn't sure where to look when Blair's voice rang out and quieted the pandemonium.

"All right, everyone. Let's clear out."

Surprisingly, no one protested. Jake grinned at his fiancé, and Daisy was unusually quiet as she stared at Officer Jameson.

Blair gave Dillon's hand a squeeze. "Don't think this is getting you out of the wedding."

He looked at Lydia and smiled. "Oh, I'll be there. You can count on it."

The blonde nodded at him, and then she and Jake left. Daisy and Jameson were still staring at each other when Dillon called the man's attention away.

As though she'd been freed from some inexplicable hold, Daisy practically ran from the room, and Lydia wanted to laugh. There was some serious chemistry between those two; she knew exactly what that felt like.

Glancing back at Dillon, she joined him and Jameson

while he finally collected Dillon's statement. Her eyes wanted to leak again as he recounted the day's events, but she blinked back the tears. There were so many emotions running through her, but the overwhelming one was relief—relief that she had the chance to spend more time with this courageous, stubborn, sexy—she grinned at the memory of him standing soaking wet and shirtless in her foyer.

Very sexy man.

The sound of Samuel's name pulled her from her thoughts. While she listened to Dillon and Jameson, it occurred to her that Samuel had given her one gift she *would* accept. Though her stalker had brought them together, Dillon was the best gift she could've asked for.

EPILOGUE

One Week Later

Dillon

Dillon ignored the dull throbbing in his chest where the bullet had torn through him. He was done with taking the prescription meds for the pain. Today was too important not to have his head on straight. Breathing deep to try and settle his nerves, he knocked on Lydia's door.

It didn't take her long to answer, and she took his breath away when she did. He'd never thought that saying was anything but an expression but seeing her in a dress that clung in all the right places made him forget to breathe.

"Wow."

She ran a nervous hand down the burnt-gold material. It was strapless, and with so much flesh exposed, the color seemed to make her olive skin glow. She'd styled her dark hair in waves past her shoulders, and her eyes seemed to shine from her artful makeup application.

"Is it too much? I didn't have many options since it was so last minute."

She was a siren, a beautiful, breathtaking creature with eyes the color of seawater that would entice any man to drown in them.

"Dillon?" She stared at him as if she was worried about something.

What did she ask me?

Thankfully, she repeated it. "It's not too much?"

He swallowed past his suddenly dry throat. "No, it's perfect. You look amazing." He had to remind himself to breathe.

At that, she finally smiled. "Thank you."

He wanted to kiss her, but he was afraid they'd never make it to the wedding if he did. And he didn't think Jake would forgive him for that.

"We should go. Now." Before he said to hell with it and showed up late to his brother's wedding.

You're the best man, you're the best man, you're the best man.

He repeated it like a mantra—or a prayer.

"Yep, we should go." He backed away from her, hoping the distance would cool him down, while she grabbed for her clutch and locked the door.

After a week on desk duty, his system was in overdrive. He'd gotten his badge and gun back along with his cramped office, but the captain barely allowed him to breathe on a report, much less take on a case until he was cleared for full duty. That was likely weeks away yet.

He had physical therapy twice a week to work his right side. It hurt like hell to grip his weapon correctly with his right hand, which was disheartening. Recovery wasn't going nearly as fast as he'd like. Added to that, he hadn't seen Lydia all week.

No wonder he was wound so tight.

He carefully climbed behind the wheel after helping her into his SUV. When he shifted into reverse, he tried not to wince as the movement sent a stab of pain straight to his chest.

At least it had the effect of settling him down . . . as long as he ignored how delicious she smelled. He wanted to lick everywhere that floral scent lingered on her body.

He took a huge breath and let it out slowly, trying to change the direction of his thoughts.

She was unusually quiet.

Glancing over, he saw her scrutinizing him. "Are you in pain?"

"Yeah," he choked out, "a little." Let her think it was his injury, not his craving for her, that was causing him to sweat.

She frowned. "Can you take something?"

"I took a couple aspirin. I'll be okay."

Reaching over, she gently squeezed his leg, and he nearly ran them off the road.

"Sorry! I didn't think I'd hurt you there."

He wanted to laugh but need edged out any other emotion.

He checked the road, then looked at her full in the face.

"You didn't." He hoped she could see the desire that was burning him up inside.

Her lips parted on an "oh," and he had to turn his eyes back to the road.

She cleared her throat; out of the corner of his vision, he saw her shift in her seat so that she sat further away from him.

You're the best man, you're the best man, you're the best—

"Well, um, you're back to work now?"

She was offering him a distraction. Good. "Yeah. Though I'm doing little more than riding a desk at the moment."

"I imagine it'll take a while to get back to full strength."

Oh, I've got enough strength for what I want to do to you.

At the thought, he nearly groaned aloud. He needed another distraction.

Tell her about Owens, that will cool your blood.

He nodded absently to himself. "I was going to tell you . . . Owens is lawyered up and going to plead insanity."

That made her frown. "They'll want me to make a statement about his mental health."

"Look, I know that's not what we wanted, but it still keeps him far away from you."

"Mm-hmm," she murmured. "I don't want to talk about him anymore tonight. I want to enjoy being on an actual date with you." She smiled, and he had to grin back at her.

But man, he wanted to kiss her.

He turned his eyes back to the road and cleared his throat. "So, how's your dad?"

"A lot better. He was released from the hospital a few days ago, and he's going to stay with me for a couple of weeks before traveling home to Greece."

"That's great. I'm glad he's doing better."

Lydia grinned at him out of the corner of his eye, "He wants to meet you properly and say thank you. Would you like to come over for dinner tomorrow?"

She was mistaken if she thought that would make him nervous. He looked forward to seeing her dad again, and hell, they'd already gotten the awkward stuff out of the way.

"Absolutely. What time?"

"Six?"

"I'll be there," he told her with a wink as he pulled up in front of the small white chapel in the middle of town.

It was a quaint wooden structure built in the mid-nineteenth century. Tall, arched windows framed a beautifully restored pair of stained wooden doors. Jake's work, Dillon knew. The steeple had been updated to metal siding over the years and was currently painted an eye-catching red. There was something decidedly cheery about the little church.

"I've always loved this church. It's a beautiful spot to get married." She smiled over at him, and he had to agree. Rolling Brook did have its charm.

As she kept smiling at him, he had a sudden vision of her decked in white floating down the aisle toward him.

He blinked and shook himself. *Seriously?*

His brother decided to tie the knot, and suddenly, he was thinking of marriage.

Should probably take her on an official date first.

He laughed aloud at himself, and she asked, "What is it?"

He shook his head. "Nothing. Shall we?"

She stared at him as if trying to read his thoughts.

With a grin, he told her, "Maybe I'll tell you someday, Doc."

An answering smile lit her face. "All right, Lieutenant."

They had to go in; it was time, but he couldn't tear his gaze away from her. "I'm crazy about you, Lydia."

Her eyes widened before she leaned in and kissed him. He held himself back, afraid of messing up her hair and makeup if he kissed her the way he wanted to.

She ended the gentle kiss. "I'm pretty fond of you too, Dillon."

Despite the pain in his chest and the ache in his groin, with Lydia grinning at him, he was beyond happy. He was exactly where he wanted to be, with exactly the woman he wanted to be with.

BONUS EPILOGUE

Four Months Later

Dillon

"You're giving her a dog for Christmas?" Dillon was hardly an expert on marriage, but he didn't think his brother had thought this through.

"Not a dog. A puppy. Blair didn't have pets growing up; besides, it's past time the farm had a mascot again."

Whiteford Farm hadn't had a dog living on it in years, since before Jake took it over from their father when Red, the shaggy collie mix he'd loved like a child, passed away at the ripe old age of seventeen.

"So really, you're getting yourself a dog in the guise of a present for Blair," he smirked at his older brother as he put the truck in park.

Jake looked taken aback as if he hadn't realized that's what he was doing. He ran a hand through his dark, shaggy hair and turned worried gray eyes on Dillon. "Shit. Do you think she'll see it like that?"

He laughed. "Yeah, she's a smart woman. Better get some jewelry to go with the pup."

When he climbed out of Jake's pickup, a blast of icy wind hit him. His hair was dark like his brother's but cut short. It offered no protection from the gusts, and he regretted not wearing a watch cap.

"Man, it's cold."

"It's December, Dill. You might not be so cold if you wore a coat." Jake joined him on the sidewalk and glanced up.

It was midafternoon, but the sky was overcast; no rays of sun shone through the clouds to help combat the icy wind.

Scratching at the stubble on his chin, Jake mused, "Bet it snows tonight. I feel it in the air."

"I *am* wearing a coat. Just because I don't parade around in long johns and flannel like some cowboy doesn't mean I'm not dressed for the cold."

His brother often wore thermals and flannel underneath his down-lined jacket, and he didn't take offense. Instead, Jake made a show of picking at Dillon's sleeve. "What is this, vinyl?"

He shrugged his brother's hand off and glared at him with sharp blue eyes. "This is department-issued for cold weather."

It was supposed to be suitable for temperatures as low as ten degrees Fahrenheit, but that was either a bogus claim or didn't account for wind chill based on the lack of warmth it was providing him currently.

"Well, I don't know who's in charge of that, but I think they need to reevaluate," Jake called after him.

He ignored the gibe and started walking ahead. They were on their way to Levi's, the jewelry store in town.

Christmas was a little over a week away, and everywhere you looked, from the streetlamps to the store windows, was decorated with wreaths, twinkling lights, and tinsel. Rolling Brook became busier this time of year. The stores that lined the main street were doing good business as shoppers hunted down those last-minute Christmas gifts.

Dillon had already bought all his gifts, apart from one—the one they were headed to pick out.

Despite the increased activity, he didn't mind the holidays, but he did mind the chill of winter. He much preferred summer's heat to this.

Regretting not wearing gloves, he shoved his hands in his pockets and hunched his shoulders against the wind that seemed to bite straight through his coat.

Damn Jake for being right.

He hoped his brother was wrong about the snow, though. He was looking forward to some time off and spending it with Lydia. If it snowed, there were bound to be traffic accidents and people needing to be rescued because they'd decided to brave the roads in their front-wheel drive vehicles.

It happened every year, but they never learned. There was a reason he drove his SUV in the winter and not the police cruiser.

The sound of someone laying on their car horn pulled

Dillon up short. He glanced toward the sound and found Mr. Delacourt waving frantically at his brother, who'd stopped a few feet behind him.

As Mr. D. pulled his giant green Oldsmobile over, Dillon followed Jake to the curb.

"Boy, am I glad I caught you!" Mr. Delacourt wheezed as if he'd been running after them instead of driving.

But the man was in his seventies. The lack of breath was probably from the excitement vibrating off him. He'd knocked his ball cap askew, and white tufts of hair stuck out from under it.

"What's going on, Mr. D.?" Jake asked.

"I was just at the diner, and Daisy said you were looking to get a dog for Christmas. As it happens, my neighbor's spaniel had a litter a couple months ago. They've got two pups they're still looking to send to a good home."

Dillon relaxed his shoulders; he'd tensed when the old man had flagged them down. His police instincts had gone on alert, but now he struggled to hold back a laugh. It wasn't unusual for Mr. Delacourt to know everyone's business. The man practically lived at Shug's Diner, where Daisy worked, and that place was a hot spot for the gossipmongers.

If Jake wanted the dog to be a secret, their sister mentioning it to Mr. D. wasn't likely to keep it that way.

"Ah, that'd be great, Mr. D. Thank you."

"Here." The elderly gentleman leaned over as far as he could with the seatbelt restraining him.

Jake reached in through the open car window to grab the piece of paper Mr. D. offered.

"I wrote the information down for you. Give 'em a call. The pups are right, pretty little things."

"I will. Thanks again." Before Mr. Delacourt could drive away, Jake stopped him. "Oh, and Mr. D.? It's supposed to be a surprise for Blair. So, if you don't mind . . . keep this between us?"

Mr. Delacourt grinned. "I won't spoil it for her."

"Thank you."

Pulling back into the street, he gave a wave while Jake tucked the paper into a pocket and turned to him.

He couldn't help the smirk. "Good luck keeping that a secret now."

Jake just shrugged. "I'm not worried about Mr. D."

At that, Dillon laughed. "No, I think it's Daisy you have to worry about."

"Yeah,"—his brother rubbed the back of his neck—"you're probably right."

"Well, at least the jewelry will be a surprise. Come on. It's freezing." Dillon resumed the walk to the corner where the jewelry store stood.

Levi's was a family-owned business, and it comprised the first two levels of a converted Victorian-era building like many of the shops along Rolling Brook's main street.

His apartment was only a few minutes away. Still, he'd ridden over with Jake because it was too cold to walk. He'd enlisted his brother's help since Jake had already been through this.

Of course, Dillon hadn't counted on the town being busy enough that they'd had to park blocks away from the shop. He gritted his teeth against the cold and kept moving. His stomach became a ball of nerves when they reached the bright blue building with its gold-painted window sign.

This was it. He was really doing this.

Jake stopped beside him. "What are we waiting on? Is the door locked?"

He shook his head at Jake's questions but couldn't pull his eyes away from the words on the window. The store's usual slogan had been erased and a new one painted on.

Put a ring on her hand this holiday season.

That's what he wanted to do, didn't he? Dillon knew Lydia was the one for him, and he thought she felt the same way. But . . . was it too soon? She'd been through a lot recently dealing with her stalker. Was he pushing her? Should he wait?

"Earth to Dillon." Jake smacked him on the back of the head and broke him out of his reverie.

He flinched and glared at his brother. "Bastard."

Jake had the nerve to shrug. "You looked like you needed it. Are we doing this or what?"

When he glanced at the window, instead of throwing back a smart-ass remark, Jake squeezed his shoulder. "Hey, Dill. You love her, right?"

Looking at his older brother, he noticed the concern in his gaze. "Yeah, I do."

"You want to marry her?"

"Yes."

Jake nodded. "Then whatever else is eating at you, let it go."

"But what if—"

"No," Jake cut him off. "You can't know what's going to

happen. She could make you the happiest man alive or the angriest. But you won't know until you ask."

Taking a deep breath, he nodded. He wasn't a coward; he could ask. "Okay."

His brother slapped him on the back and grinned. "Let's go get you a ring."

* * * *

Dillon

Dillon's eyes wanted to cross. They'd spent over an hour looking at diamond rings before he'd finally settled on one. Who knew there were so damned many to choose from?

If he ever had to do this again—not that he planned to— he'd ask the woman to marry him, then make her come pick out her own ring. It had to be much less of a headache that way.

Rubbing at the one brewing at his left temple, he glanced at Jake. His brother seemed perfectly at ease as he chatted away with the saleswoman. He'd already found a pendant and a pair of earrings for Blair in the time it'd taken Dillon to pick one ring.

They'd taken the engagement ring he'd chosen to the back room, where it would be sized to fit. That had been a feat in itself, getting Lydia's ring size. Thankfully, Daisy had helped him with that, and his soon-to-be fiancé was none the wiser.

He hoped she'd like the ring. It had a simple white-gold band and a pear-shaped diamond, but the two smaller aquamarine gemstones on either side of the diamond were what made him choose it. They'd instantly reminded him of her ocean-colored eyes.

He loved her eyes, especially the way they darkened when he—*Dammit!*

Now, the saleswoman was trying to push a matching bracelet at Jake.

He wanted to growl at his brother to hurry up, but he contained himself. Instead, he sat in one of the velvet-lined chairs at the edge of the showroom. He closed his eyes and, for the first time since they'd entered, noticed the Christmas carols that played softly in the background and the smell of peppermint scenting the air.

One thing about living in a small town was that people went all in for the holidays. He wasn't a Scrooge, but it was nice when that holiday cheer meant he'd received a hefty discount on the ring he'd just bought. A cop's salary wasn't that impressive, even as a Lieutenant. Not that he minded. He was happy on the path he'd chosen.

Sure, his brother had done well for himself with his construction and carpentry work, but Jake had left Rolling Brook to do it. Dillon was happy right where he was, and he didn't need the money—he owned part of Whiteford. They all did. But he nor Daisy would ever try to sell it off. It was worth much more than money.

He'd been thinking about buying a house, though. Over the last two months, he'd spent most of his time at Lydia's, but she hadn't asked him to move in.

Dammit, maybe I am rushing things.

His hands clenched into fists and pounded on his legs. With a low growl, he popped his eyes open and shoved to his feet in one quick motion. He needed air, cold be damned.

His brother was still looking at the bracelet.

"I'll be outside, Jake."

At his statement, his brother looked up. "What? I thought you didn't like the co—"

He was out the door before Jake could finish. His head was pounding now, and the cold air was almost soothing. His blood pumped with nervous energy, and he started to pace to the end of the block as his thoughts raced back and forth.

He could wait a few months to propose. Just because he'd bought the ring didn't mean he had to give it to her right away.

No, dammit. I don't want to wait.

What he wanted was Lydia—all of her. No more going back and forth between homes and worrying if she would disappear on him. He wanted her in his bed every night and to see those beautiful siren's eyes when he woke each morning.

He loved her, and he'd never loved another woman. Sure, he'd enjoyed them. But what he felt for her wasn't easy, and damn, at the moment, it wasn't enjoyable either.

He scrubbed a hand over the ache in his chest. She had the ability to tie him up in knots with worry. He thought if she agreed to marry him, that would go away. She'd be his for good.

But what if she wasn't ready? What if she . . .

Dillon felt his throat constrict at the thought he couldn't finish; he swallowed hard to clear it.

No, that's not going to happen.

He rubbed at the throbbing in his temple and stopped pacing. Glancing around, he realized a few people had curious stares pointed in his direction. He probably looked like a junkie pacing here in the cold, mumbling to himself.

Where the hell was Jake? Was he buying the whole damned store?

Refusing to spend more time on the possibility Lydia would reject him, he stomped back to the jewelry store and wrenched the door open, causing the bells hanging from a hook in its center to jingle excitedly.

Frowning at the festive noise, he stepped inside. A blast of heat hit him, along with the tinkling of a Christmas melody.

Jake stood at the counter with his back facing the door.

"Aren't you done yet?"

At the harsh tone of his voice, Jake turned around. "Just finishing up. Don't you need your ring?"

"No. It'll take a couple days to be sized," he replied through gritted teeth.

"Oh."

"Here you are, sir." The saleswoman handed over his brother's purchases, likely too preoccupied with calculating the commission she'd earn from the sale she'd just made to notice the tension coming off of him.

"Thanks." Jake grabbed the bag without looking at the woman. He'd trained his eyes on Dillon, who probably looked ready to bite someone's head off.

As soon as his brother's hand connected with the bag, Dillon stepped back outside. He needed a drink. Or maybe a session in the ring with Jameson. He flexed his hands. Punching something sounded like a great idea. Too bad his friend was in Florida visiting family for Christmas.

"Hey, Dill." Jake caught up and stopped him with a hand on his arm. "Are you all right? I haven't seen you this worked up since . . . well, you know."

He picked up on the apprehension in Jake's voice. *Fuck.* Did he really seem as upset as he'd been when he'd been struggling to get over the death of one of his junior officers?

He didn't think he was . . . No, he'd dealt with that guilt. This was different. He was angry because the alternative was . . . *fear.*

The realization relieved some of the heat from his anger, and he sighed heavily. "I need a drink."

As far as big brothers went, Jake was a damned good one. He knew not to push. Instead, he nodded. "Okay. Let's get one."

* * * *

Dillon

It might've only been four in the afternoon, but Dillon didn't care. He was off-duty; he could have a drink if he wanted—or needed—one.

Right now, he felt like he needed it. Something to take the edge off the nerves, making his stomach roil and his pulse pound. He downed the shot of whiskey and frowned.

Damn, he had a headache. The noise in the bar wasn't helping either. He and Jake were at Nick's Tavern, a popular watering hole for the cops in town. The tavern had embraced the holiday spirit. Garland decorated the rack of bottles behind the bar, and a slim tree with multi-colored lights stood in one corner. A few other off-duties were having a cold one while they watched a replay of Thursday night's football game.

The rest of the patrons appeared to be starting the weekend early. They were already obnoxiously loud—singing along with the Christmas carols blasting out of the overhead speakers. Or maybe it just sounded like they blasted because his head was throbbing.

Sighing, he glanced at his brother from the corner of his eye. Jake sat next to him in companionable silence and nursed a beer. "Were you nervous? When you asked Blair?"

He laughed. "Of course, that's normal."

"No. I mean—you weren't worried it was too soon? That she would say no?"

His brother gave a slight shrug. "Not really. We loved each other. Why would she say no?"

He frowned at Jake's response. "Well, had you talked about it? I mean, some women aren't into marriage, right? How'd you know she'd accept?"

His brother scratched at his chin. "Ah, no, we hadn't discussed it, but that might've been smart. Look, Dill"—he turned on his stool—"you can't know 100 percent that Lydia will say yes, but what's got you so worried she won't?"

Good question. Why am I so worried?

As a cop, he was used to following his gut, so what was making him determined to doubt her commitment?

Dillon scrubbed a hand across his five o'clock shadow.

She'd been acting . . . off. He couldn't pinpoint what it was, but something wasn't quite the same with her. "I don't know."

Jake reached across the space between them and gave him a soft pat on the back. "If it helps, I've seen you two together. I don't think you have anything to worry about."

His brother eased a bit of the worry, but something still nagged him. "Thanks." Dillon stood. "We should probably—"

The door to the tavern flew open and smacked the wall with a bang loud enough to make his ears ring.

Dammit!

Not only did that not help his head, but the cold air that blew in only served to sour his mood more. To top it off, no one was there. The cursed thing had blown open from the gust because whoever had left last didn't pull the door all the way closed. It was an old wooden monstrosity that didn't latch half the time.

Everyone in the tavern had turned toward the front door, but no one moved to close it. Swearing under his breath, he threw cash on the bar and shrugged into his coat. Gesturing for Jake to follow, he headed for the exit.

As they stepped outside in the waning light, he cursed again. It was starting to snow.

"Wish you'd been wrong about the snow," he grumbled and hunched his shoulders against the gusts that blew flakes into his face.

Jake grinned. "Come on, now, brother. A white Christmas would be nice."

"Sure it would when half the town loses power, and I

end up working to rescue idiots who try to brave the roads." He shook his head at his brother before he climbed into the truck. "Hurry up, will you? I'm driving out to Lydia's tonight." The snow hadn't improved his temper, but he knew seeing her would.

Jake chuckled and climbed into the driver's seat. "You're just a regular Grinch today."

"Yeah. I guess I am." He cranked up the heat to full blast as Jake turned the truck toward his apartment.

With his fingers finally warming up, he hoped the snow didn't get too heavy before he made it out to Lydia's. Her house was only a few minutes outside of town in an older neighborhood, but the plows wouldn't be out that way until tomorrow morning at the earliest. Not that he'd mind being snowed in with her for the weekend . . .

No, he wouldn't mind that at all. Dillon's sulk slightly lifted as he fantasized about having her to himself all weekend.

As Jake pulled into a parking spot in front of the historic brick building that housed a sandwich shop and Dillon's one-bedroom apartment, he admitted he was glad his brother had been with him today. He still wasn't sure why he was so worried that Lydia would turn him down, but having Jake to bounce his fears off had helped.

Turning in his seat, he cleared his throat. "Thank you for coming with me today."

His brother smiled before giving a curt nod. "Anytime, Dill."

He felt some of the tension squeezing his head like a vise dissipate. With a nod in response, Dillon climbed out of the pickup. "Drive safe."

"You too."

With a wave, Dillon hurried into his apartment. He needed to get on the road to Lydia's before the snow piled up.

* * * *

Lydia

Lydia hunched her shoulders as she leaned in close to her laptop. She'd kicked off her heels but had yet to change out of her work clothes. Excitement had her bouncing her black-stockinged feet.

She didn't often work from home, which meant the room she'd turned into an office saw little activity—usually. But she was busy plotting tonight.

Once the idea had struck, she'd had to act on it. It had taken her a few days of snooping through Dillon's calendar to figure out the best timing, but she'd finally settled on the perfect dates—she hoped.

Biting her overly full lip in concentration, she strained closer to the screen. Her dark brown hair fell over her shoulder as she squinted her eyes to read the flight details she scrolled through.

A slow smile spread across her face and lit her sea-green eyes as she found what she was looking for—departure from Chicago O'hare International to Thessaloniki, Greece, with only one layover.

Perfect. Now, all she needed to do was book it.

She was so engrossed in what was on the screen in front

of her that she jerked and let out a squeal as strong hands landed on her shoulders.

"I'm sorry I scared you, beautiful. I thought you would've heard me come in." Dillon leaned down and placed a kiss on her cheek. "What are you working on?"

She panicked as he moved to peek around her shoulder and slammed the laptop lid down. "Nothing. Um, that is, nothing exciting. Just some notes from work. Client confidentiality, you know." She shrugged and smiled, hoping he'd buy her excuse.

It wouldn't be unusual for her to have confidential notes on a client. She was a therapist, but . . . she rarely brought her work home with her.

Before he had a chance to doubt her, she stood and hooked her arms around his neck. "Hi."

Doing her best to distract him, she pushed her breasts into his chest as she pulled his head down for a kiss. Teasing him, she nipped his bottom lip, then soothed it with her tongue.

He responded with a low growl as his hands cupped her bottom and pulled her closer to him. She moaned and deepened the kiss, sweeping her tongue into his mouth to tantalize as well as taste. It was warm and smoky like the whiskey he'd had not long before.

Running her hands over his shoulders and then down his back, she savored the feel of him. It had become familiar, but it still excited her.

As the kiss continued, all thoughts of distracting him fled. She was lost in him and wanted more. Gripping his shirt in her hands, she was ready to lift it over his head when he pulled back, breaking the spell. She let out a small groan in frustration and frowned.

Chuckling, he cupped her face in his hands as he leaned his forehead against hers. "That was some hello."

Desire had caused a fog in her brain, which took a moment to lift. When it did, she smiled coyly. "Well, it was going to be a bit more."

Dillon released her with a grin. "Did you know it was snowing?"

"What? Really! It's the first of the season."

"Mm-hmm," he murmured as she bounced on her toes with excitement.

She loved the first snow of winter. There was something magical about it when the flakes floated down like little stars settling onto the earth to create a pristine white blanket. "I want to see it!"

Forgetting she wasn't dressed for the cold in her white blouse and khaki pencil skirt, Lydia practically ran down the hall to her front door. Once there, she wrenched it open, and a blast of frosty air hit her. She shivered and laughed at herself as Dillon's arms came around her from behind.

"I know you love it, but I'm dreading the phone calls it's sure to bring tomorrow."

"What do you mean?" she watched the flurries swirl in the wind before they made their way to the ground.

It was cold enough that they would stick, but with him holding her, she didn't mind the chill.

"I checked the weather. We're supposed to get a foot or more. People venturing out in it will either get stuck and need a rescue, or they'll cause traffic accidents. Happens every year. Not sure why they can't stay home until the roads have been plowed."

She felt him shake his head at the statement. Turning in his arms, she stretched up and kissed him lightly. "Well, I certainly don't mind being snowed in with you."

As his crooked grin appeared, her heart swelled. She loved that grin and was happy she'd cleared his frustration over the weather.

"I'm glad you feel that way because I've got a surprise for you."

"Oh? And what might that be?" She tried to look stern; he knew she wasn't fond of surprises, but, in truth, she didn't mind them so much when they came from Dillon.

Excitement bubbled in her chest at the thought of her own surprise for him. His arrival had been horrible timing. Now she'd have to search for the tickets again and hope they were still available.

"Close your eyes." She raised an eyebrow, and he warned, "I'll blindfold you if I need to."

Huffing out a breath at his threat, she complied and closed her eyes. "Just what are you up to, Lieutenant?"

He closed the front door and grabbed her hand. Then he started to lead her in the direction of the living room.

When he paused her, she dutifully kept her eyes shut, though the temptation to peek was extreme. "Can I open them yet?"

"Not yet." Dillon placed his hands on her shoulders and turned her ninety degrees. "The couch is behind you, okay? Sit, but keep your eyes closed."

She reached back with a hand and connected with what she knew was the deep purple velvet of her living room couch. Satisfied she wouldn't fall, she sat down as she heard rustling in the direction of the fireplace.

She smiled as she listened to the gas turning on and the flame igniting. "Ooh, that'll be nice."

"Hey, eyes closed, Doc."

She chuckled at him. "I didn't open them, Lieutenant." She emphasized his rank since he'd called her 'Doc.' They only used the titles in playful banter now.

Last summer, when he was her client, seemed years ago as opposed to only months. She'd even taken her own advice with his urging. She saw a counselor regularly to work through her experiences with Samuel and the scars it left behind. Those emotional demons bothered her less every day, and she knew she had Dillon to thank for that.

She heard him move her coffee table, and then the sound of a cloth whipping out made her jump. "What are you up to?"

She was met with silence, and several seconds ticked by.

"Okay, open them," he whispered in her ear.

Smiling as his hot breath tickled her, Lydia opened her eyes. "Oh!" she gasped. Her gaze flew to Dillon's. "You . . ." She looked back at her living room floor. "Oh!" A hand came up to cover her mouth.

He'd pushed the coffee table and the other couch aside to make room for a red and green plaid blanket with a picnic basket and a wine chiller with her favorite white wine.

Overcome, she threw her arms around him and planted kisses on his cheeks. "Thank you, Dillon. This is such a good surprise. I love it!"

His dark blue eyes glowed like sapphires as they met hers. "You're welcome. I wanted to make the most of our night in."

She felt warmth flood her body at the meaning behind his words. With a swallow, she looked away before she kissed him again, and they missed out on the thoughtful surprise he'd just given her.

"So, what's in this picnic you've prepared?" She moved to sit on the blanket, then snuggled closer to the fire as she missed his warmth.

He grinned his crooked grin as if he knew why she'd moved away. "Let me show you."

He joined her on the blanket and began to unload the dinner he'd gathered for them. It was a feast of her favorite foods. There was an array of charcuterie: salami, several hard kinds of cheese, grapes, and kalamata olives.

She smiled as he continued to place dishes in front of her. Next was a pasta salad with feta cheese, tomatoes, and cucumber. Her mouth salivated, but he only grinned, not yet finished. The last thing in the basket was a blueberry cheesecake. That dessert was special because her mother had always made it for her birthday.

Her heart warmed at his thoughtfulness, but really, it was too much food for just the two of them.

She laughed at the massive amount, which nearly covered the entire blanket. "How long did you think we'd be snowed in for?"

"I'm hoping all weekend, and as much as I love these tight skirts of yours"—he trailed a finger up her thigh, and she shivered—"I don't think you're going to need them." He winked, then leaned forward to nip the lip she was chewing on.

Pulling back, she raised an eyebrow. "What?" She gulped as she continued to stare into his eyes. Those deep blue pools told her he had plans for them this weekend, which didn't involve getting out of bed.

"I'll show you later."

She licked her lips in anticipation as his words fanned the flames of her desire.

Mm, I love the snow.

She grinned when he poured her a glass of wine into a festive plastic cup. This was going to be a fantastic weekend.

* * * *

Lydia

Hours later, they lay naked in each other's arms in front of the fire, enjoying the soft sound of the blower as it hummed in the background. Lydia smiled at the flames dancing around the faux logs. Her head lay on Dillon's chest, and she stroked his skin with her palm, enjoying the ridges his muscles made as she trailed her hand back and forth.

This year had been an eventful one, and despite its ups and downs, she wouldn't change any of it because it had led her to Rolling Brook and him. Over the last few months, she'd gotten closer to Dillon and his family. His siblings were now good friends of hers.

She still couldn't quite believe how welcoming they'd been—absorbing her into their circle as if she'd been a part of it all along. It felt unbelievably good; she hadn't realized how lonely she'd been since her father had moved to Greece.

Seeing Dillon's parents and knowing how close all the Redlands were, she felt so lucky to be a part of their lives as well as his. They'd been spending any free time they had together. Most nights, he ended up staying at her house.

Perhaps it was time she invited him to stay permanently . . . but she worried he would feel pressured or think it was too soon. She knew his relationship history—or lack of it— and the last thing she wanted was to do anything that would cause him to pull away.

He had her heart, and she didn't want to think about what would happen to it if she scared him off. Her hand paused over his chest. His breathing had fallen into a regular rhythm, and she raised her head to look at him.

He was asleep. With his features relaxed, the usual stern demeanor of his brow softened, and he seemed peaceful. She knew something was weighing on him, but she hadn't wanted to push him. He'd tell her when he was ready. And she would help him through it.

Just as she'd done a few months ago.

Watching his breathing, remembering how she'd agonized over it in the hospital after he'd been shot, she placed a soft kiss over his heart. "I love you, Dillon."

Content, she snuggled back into the crook of his arm and closed her eyes.

The warm afternoon sun glinted off the bright white of the boat they'd rented as Dillon sailed them into a secluded cove. Lydia shielded her eyes as she took in the view from her spot in the bow.

The beautiful turquoise water of the Aegean Sea sparkled, and her heart soared. Something about the waters off Thessaloniki called to her, and she was overjoyed to share it with him.

While coming to Greece was a dream vacation, it felt like coming home. She'd missed visiting in the summer like she'd done as a child with her mother and Baba.

Remembering those summers, she vowed to make this a regular visit for her and Dillon. She grinned at the thought and turned to watch him as he readied the anchor. He was shirtless, and the sun made his copper skin glow.

As he worked the winch, his muscles straining, she felt heat settle in her core and licked her lips. She'd never get tired of looking at this man.

With the anchor lowered, he straightened and glanced over at her. Catching the lustful expression she knew was on her face, he grinned and advanced.

"You shouldn't look at me like that, Doc." Dillon reached for her, pushing the strands of hair the breeze blew loose behind her ear.

"Like how, Lieutenant?" She widened her eyes—the picture of innocence.

He chuckled. "You truly are a siren."

She grinned, and before she knew what was happening, he'd crushed her to him in a kiss that staggered her. Half in a daze, she placed her hands on his shoulders. The feel of his bare skin under her palms was deliciously warm and wet from the spray. He smelled salty like the sea.

She hummed in appreciation, but the sound was muffled as he plundered her mouth. His hands roamed over her bare skin until he found the clasp of her monokini. She felt it give way, and the halter straps slid down her chest, exposing her breasts. The breeze tickled her skin and set her nerve endings alight.

Dillon released her lips and trailed kisses down her neck. She moaned as he continued his exploration and captured a taut nipple in his mouth. When he nibbled at it with his teeth, she gasped, the sting of both pleasure and pain roaring through her.

He continued suckling, and his mouth was driving her crazy. "Dillon."

He released her breast and pushed her suit the rest of the way down. "What do you want, Lydia? Tell me."

Her chest rose and fell with her rapid breaths. He'd made her needy so quickly. "You. I want you."

She reached for his swim trunks and struggled to tug them over the bulge that had grown there. A growl of frustration escaped her lips, and he chuckled before helping her take them off him.

She drank in his hard length before wrapping her fingers around it. As she began to move her hand up and down, he groaned and captured her mouth again.

Walking her backward to the bench seat in the bow, he lowered her onto it. The cushion gave way under their combined weight, and he captured her hands above her head. She flexed them, trying to break free.

When he wouldn't release her, she pouted; she wanted to touch him.

"Not so fast, Doc. We'll just keep these pretty little hands up here for now." He moved his free hand lower, and as he kissed her again, she decided she didn't mind being captured.

As one then two fingers entered her, Lydia bucked against his hand, wanting more.

She broke the kiss to plead. "More, Dillon. I want more."

He grinned down at her before positioning himself between her legs. Lydia moaned in anticipation and welcomed the stretch as he filled her. Their eyes connected. His were as dark as the deepest ocean depths; she drowned in them as he moved in and out of her in a slow rhythm that matched the boat's rocking.

The urgency she'd felt washed away until she floated on a sea of sensation. Love as warm as the sun on their skin poured out of her in waves. She'd only ever felt like this with him. He was her everything.

He kissed her as the pleasure built in soft waves. Soon, they'd pull her under.

When his hand reached between their bodies, she cried out and—

Lydia opened her eyes to see the ceiling of her living room.

Ugh, what a horrible time to wake up!

She squeezed her thighs together with a groan. That dream had been . . . so real. At least, she found they were still lying on her living room floor as she fully awoke.

Grinning now, she reached for Dillon under the blanket;

she'd get to finish her dream. And in a couple of months, she'd make it a reality.

* * * *

Unknown

While Lydia brought her dream to life, another worked on making his own dreams come true. Across town, a young man punched in a four-digit code to disarm an old Victorian building. A huge grin split his face as he heard the beep that confirmed he'd put in the right combination.

Using the dim glow from his penlight, he grabbed the keys that hung on a hook by the back door and followed the hall to the showroom at its end.

His eyes adjusted to the soft light streaming in from the front window when he stepped inside. He'd dressed all in black, but his eyes weren't the only thing that gleamed as he took in the enormous amount of wealth displayed in the locked cases.

Diamonds and gemstones winked at him; they were all his—his for the taking. Running his gloved fingers across the glass, he released a low whistle in awe and got to work.

* * * *

Dillon

Yesterday, it had taken Dillon longer than he'd anticipated to grab a few supplies before heading over to Lydia's. The town had already gone on high alert at the snowstorm threat, and half the local market had been relieved of its goods.

You'd think people had never seen snow before, the way they went into such a panic, even though it happened every winter in this part of Illinois. Thankfully, Lydia had plenty of coffee, and he didn't have to brave the foot and a half of snow that had fallen throughout the evening to procure more.

He stood staring at the pot on her kitchen counter, willing the thing to brew faster. They'd made their way to her bedroom sometime during the early morning hours, but he slept poorly afterward. His mind wouldn't let go of how she'd slammed her laptop when he'd surprised her yesterday.

She was hiding something, and it made him uneasy.

He ran his fingers through his dark hair as he thought about it. Maybe it really was work, but his gut told him otherwise.

Sighing, he rolled his neck and shook off the uncertainty. Now wasn't the time to worry over it. He wanted to take advantage of each second he had with her, all to himself.

He hadn't minded the wake-up she'd given him earlier. That had been worth every sleepless minute that came after. He didn't know what had worked her into such a state, but he was happy to consider it an early Christmas gift.

Thank you, Santa.

Grinning at the memory, he reached for two mugs. The muscles in his bare back stretched as he grabbed them from the upper cabinet. He was wearing only boxers, and after he took a sip of the warm brew, it sent a shiver through him. The house held a chill, and standing barefoot on the kitchen's tile floor wasn't helping. He knew the perfect way to warm up, though.

After pouring Lydia a cup of coffee, Dillon carried the mugs back to her bedroom with a wicked grin on his face.

* * * *

Dillon

A few hours later, after Dillon had repaid Lydia with a wake-up call of his own, they sat on the loveseat on her back porch, wrapped in a heavy blanket while they enjoyed another cup of coffee. The hills that stretched beyond her backyard were snow-covered and, as yet, still untouched.

She shivered beside him, and he reached an arm around her to draw her in closer. It was below freezing and probably too cold to sit outside, but she'd wanted to see the snow.

He found it adorable the way she got so excited about it.

"It's so pretty when it's like this." She snuggled into him as she spoke.

"It is."

Mindful of what Jake had said, Dillon was trying not to ruin her happiness by acting like the Grinch. It was almost Christmas, after all.

Despite the chill, he was warm and cozy, with her head leaning against his shoulder. Being with her like this made the outside world fade away. It was as good as the time they'd spent together in the bedroom.

He grinned—well, nearly as good.

Enjoying the smell of gardenia that always hung on her skin, he nuzzled her neck. He was contemplating whether they would freeze if he took her on the loveseat when she straightened and tilted her head as though straining to hear something.

"What are you doing?"

"Do you hear that?"

He was clueless; his concentration, along with his blood, had flowed south. "Hear what?"

"Sounds like beeping."

This time, he heard it. "That's my phone! Be right back." He kissed the top of Lydia's head and jumped up to answer his cell.

Racing back to the bedroom, Dillon managed to grab his phone off the nightstand right as it stopped ringing. "Dammit!"

When he unlocked it, he looked at the missed call notification. It was the station.

Well, that can't be good.

Grumbling, he hit redial and waited for the line to connect.

"Rolling Brook Police—"

"It's Lieutenant Redland. What's going on?" He sat on the edge of the bed, head drooping as he dreaded the answer. He was sure his alone time with Lydia was about to end.

"Oh, right. Sir, we've had a 10-27, likely 10-96."

He almost rolled his eyes at the response from the rookie on dispatch. Newbies loved to use 10 codes, which wouldn't be a problem, except the young cop had told him there'd been a break-in and a theft but not where it had happened or what was taken.

Knowing this meant ending his quiet weekend with Lydia, he couldn't help the sarcasm. "At the station!" he exclaimed, mock-alarmed.

"What? No, ah, sir. It was at Levi's, the jeweler in town."

"Levi's?" Damn, that wasn't good. What if they got Lydia's ring?

His stomach roiled at the thought, and he swallowed against the bile that wanted to rise in his throat.

"Yes, sir." No longer able to contain his excitement over this kind of crime happening in their sleepy little town, the rookie was full of details. "Happened last night during the storm. It knocked the power out in town, and the crews are still working on it. Looks like someone took advantage of the alarm being down. There's a patrol on the way, but the captain said you could get there quicker with you living in town."

"Yeah, well, I'm not in town." Dillon sighed; he'd thought someone had gotten stuck or in an accident at worse. A burglary? That was a whole other level of bad.

"Oh, um, okay, sir. I can tell the captain—"

"Don't worry about it, rook. I'm on my way." His relationship with the captain was still a tenuous one. He didn't need another reason to piss off the man.

"All right. Thanks, Lieutenant. The owners are there waiting to catalog what was stolen."

"10-4." He disconnected and fought the urge to throw his phone.

Dammit! This was not how he pictured this weekend going.

Growling in frustration, he rose and grabbed his shoulder holster off Lydia's dresser. He slipped it on with a sigh—time to tell her that duty called.

* * * *

Dillon

The last theft in Rolling Brook had been small potatoes compared to this one. Someone completely emptied the jewelry store. They'd even taken the loose gemstones from the workroom.

Dillon frowned as he walked around the empty cases. There was nothing left to sparkle and shine. Lydia's ring had been part of the haul, which only soured his mood more.

Having been at Levi's for the last four hours, he was tired and cranky. The two police officers from the department trained in forensics had dusted the place for latent fingerprints. Everything had been wiped clean, which meant this had been a professional or, at least, someone who knew how to cover their tracks.

Dillon sipped a cup of coffee some brave soul had offered him despite the scowl that had taken over his face. He paced as he went over all they knew. The power outage had knocked out the main alarm, but the backup had been working. Whoever had broken in knew the code to disarm it. That told him they were dealing with a local or at least someone with a local connection.

He already had the owners compiling a list of all the employees they'd had over the last year, which was the last time they'd changed the code. He shook his head at that. Having insurance was one thing, but you'd think they'd have tighter security with the amount of product they kept on hand.

All told, over 200,000 dollars in wholesale value had been stolen. With retail markup, the thieves would be looking at a lot more.

At this point, it was the largest case of larceny Rolling Brook had ever seen. The catalog of stolen jewelry pieces was extensive. If the burglars were smart, they wouldn't try to sell it anywhere nearby. With the complete list in hand, he'd already given the order to distribute it to local jewelers and pawn shops on the off chance whoever had stolen the items would be dumb enough to try and get rid of them that way.

Downing the rest of his coffee, he pinched the bridge of his nose. He had a headache brewing there. The theft was a misfortune for the town, but he had a personal stake in recovering the stolen goods. He needed Lydia's ring back, or he didn't know what he was going to do. Proposing without it wasn't an option, at least not for him.

Is this a sign?

He hadn't been able to rid himself of the fear he was moving too fast. Maybe the ring disappearing was a sign. If she wasn't even ready for him to live with her, getting engaged might be a step too far. He didn't want to lose her.

Perhaps he should buy that house first and ask her to move in with *him.* Then, he'd propose . . . later. And with a different ring.

He stood frowning at nothing as his thoughts once again revolved around whether or not he should propose to Lydia.

"Here are the names, Lieutenant." An officer shoved a folder at him, breaking him out of his rumination.

He glanced down at the folder that held the list of employees. "Thanks."

The officer clapped him on the back. His excitement was as apparent as the rookie's on the phone had been. "Time to make some house calls."

Sighing, Dillon opened the door to the jewelry store. He hunched his shoulders against the cold and trudged through the snow with heavy footsteps on the way to his SUV.

At least this list wasn't that long. It only had ten names, and he might even be able to get through all of them today. He hoped he could, but his luck had been nonexistent so far.

* * * *

Dillon

Dillon pulled into a park in front of the aging apartment complex on the outskirts of town. He cracked his neck from side to side, but it did little to ease the tension that had set up shop there. He was at the residence of the last employee on the list, and it was nearly seven o'clock. His stomach growled, but he ignored it.

The only stop he'd made as he'd worked his way through the names had been for coffee. The lack of real food wasn't helping his mood because none of the employees he'd talked to had seemed the slightest bit suspicious. He was quickly coming to a dead end.

Scowling at the lack of real progress on the case, he climbed out of his SUV and sunk into a foot of snow. He cursed as the cold, wet powder entered the top of his boots. Slamming the car door, he stomped to the stairs leading to the second level. Thankfully, someone had swept them off and made the climb easier on him. He was searching for 2B and the last name on his list.

Finding the correct apartment, he knocked sharply on the door and hoped like hell the woman was home.

The door opened to reveal a girl of maybe twenty with long blonde hair and big blue eyes—a regular Pollyanna. "Yes?"

"Are you Zoey Boone?"

"I am."

"I'm sure you've heard about the break-in at Levi's?" The young woman nodded, so he continued, "I'm Lieutenant Redland with the Rolling Brook Police. We're speaking with all of the employees. Can I come in?"

He wanted to get this over with as soon as possible, and questioning her inside, out of the cold, was preferable.

"Of course, Lieutenant." Zoey stepped back and opened the door wide.

He felt the temperature change immediately and nearly sighed in relief when he stepped inside. He needed to invest in some warmer clothes.

They moved to the two club chairs in her tiny living room, and he began questioning her about the night of the theft. Five minutes in, his heart sank. She seemed open and friendly and hardly capable of stealing her employer's entire inventory.

"Miss Boone, have you ever shared the alarm code with anyone—even inadvertently—that you're aware of?" He'd expected an immediate "no," so when the young woman's face flushed and she looked away from his gaze, he sat up a little straighter, ready to press her if need be. "Miss Boone?"

She cleared her throat but continued to look at her lap. "I think so. That is, there was this one time—a few months ago, I . . . "

When she trailed off and started fidgeting, he leaned closer. "What happened a few months ago, Miss Boone?" His voice was stern and authoritative. He needed her to answer him.

She winced before explaining, "I went in after-hours with my boyfriend. I wanted to show him the pieces I loved, and he suggested we go after closing. He wanted to, that is, ah, well"—as she stammered, her face turned completely red—"we made love in my boss's office."

The young woman looked up at him then, and her next words flowed out in a rush. "She's such a bitch to me, and it was just for fun. I know I'm not supposed to be in there after closing, but it was just for that. We didn't touch any of the cases, I promise. Please, Lieutenant, don't tell Mr. Levi. I can't lose my job!"

Despite what she looked like, this girl was no Pollyanna. He almost felt sorry for her—almost. "Look, Miss Boone, I'm here to find the thief, nothing more. What happens with your employer is out of my hands. I need to know your boyfriend's name. Now."

Tears flooded her eyes. "He's gone. I haven't heard from him in days. He just ghosted me"—her voice hiccupped—"after everything." She sighed, and a tear tracked down her cheek.

Dillon wasn't about to let the waterworks sway him. "His name, Miss Boone."

She glanced back down at her lap and mumbled, "Jesse Laudabaker."

Dammit! That kid was a pain in Dillon's ass. If Laudabaker was behind this, and all signs pointed to his involvement, he would make sure the punk did time for this. Juvie clearly hadn't taught him any lessons.

"Thank you, Miss Boone." Shoving to his feet, Dillon warned, "Don't go anywhere. And if Mr. Laudabaker makes contact, you call me right away."

The poor girl was in tears, but he ignored them and handed her his information. "I'll let myself out."

* * * *

Dillon

Dillon sat frowning at his computer screen after the calendar notification reminded him that Christmas was two days away. Two days and no leads. No leads meant no ring.

Frustrated with the lack of progress in finding Jesse Laudabaker, Dillon shoved to his feet and started pacing within the boundaries of his small station office. The kid had vanished. They'd already checked his usual haunts, and he'd even gone to have a chat with his former foster family. But it had all provided nothing. Nothing to lead them to wherever the young criminal was hiding.

He didn't have proof that Laudabaker had taken the jewelry, but Dillon knew it in his gut. The real question was whether the punk had stolen the jewelry for someone else or if he knew how to offload it himself. However, Dillon doubted that.

Laudabaker hadn't proved to be the brightest a few years ago when he'd failed to notice the security cameras Shug had installed after the first round of car break-ins in her parking lot. The kid had been a jaded sixteen-year-old when Dillon first busted him. Now, he'd graduated from car stereos to a major jewelry heist.

His hands clenched into fists as he continued to pace. At this point, he wouldn't likely get Lydia's ring back in time for Christmas. Hell, if that wasn't a sign, how she'd acted so secretive lately was reason enough to wait on the proposal.

Running a restless hand through his hair, he paused in his pacing. What was Lydia hiding? Just yesterday, he'd borrowed her phone to check his personal email since he didn't like to do that on his official cell, and she'd almost had a conniption when he'd accessed the email app. It had opened to her inbox, and she'd immediately snatched the phone away.

He respected her privacy and wouldn't have gone through her emails, but it had surprised him that she'd reacted that way. She'd never attempted to hide things from him before.

Slumping onto the edge of his desk, Dillon sighed. He wished he knew what was going on with her. His desk phone rang and interrupted his thoughts.

Reaching for the receiver, answered absently, "Redland."

"Lieutenant, we've just had a call from . . ."—there was a pause as the officer on the line glanced down at his notes—"Bunker's Cash for Pawn. The caller said he's got a ring that matches one stolen from Levi's."

Dillon launched himself off the desk, and his grip on the phone increased as hope that it could be Lydia's ring bubbled up in his chest.

The officer was still talking. "He said he'd try and stall the young man wanting to sell it, but if you want to catch him—"

"I'm on it. Text me the address," Dillon barked and hung up the phone.

He grabbed his coat off the back of his chair and slung it on as he raced out the station's door. He was determined not to lose this opportunity in case the young man was Laudabaker.

* * * *

Dillon

Dillon sped to a stop in front of the pawn shop. The

building was a low rectangular thing with faded brick and a big front glass window. It had taken him only minutes to arrive despite the business being in a neighboring town.

Using his lights and siren, he'd gone faster than was safe on the snowy roads, but he wasn't about to blow this chance at catching the kid.

Climbing quickly from his SUV, he pulled his weapon and held it low as he approached the entrance. Through the storefront's glass, he could see that the clerk had a man with brown hair who looked the right height and build, engaged in conversation at the counter.

Good. Made it in time.

Dillon took a deep breath and shoved the door open with his boot. "Jesse Laudabaker."

At the sound of the name, the man swung around. It was Laudabaker, all right. When he saw Dillon, his brown eyes widened, and he shifted to reach for a weapon.

"Don't move! Put your hands up where I can see them." Dillon raised his firearm and pointed it at Laudabaker's chest.

The punk made him nervous; he didn't want to get shot again. It had hurt like a son-of-a-bitch the last time, and his right side was finally starting to feel normal. The kid's eyes bounced around the shop, looking for an escape route.

Approaching slowly, he kept his sight on Laudabaker while he spoke to the man behind the counter. "Where's the ring?"

The pawn shop clerk picked it up and held it where Dillon could get a good look at it. It had a white-gold band

and a setting with a pear-shaped diamond and two aquamarine gemstones.

Yep, that's Lydia's ring.

Knowing he'd just solved the case, his heart raced in excitement. "Turn around slowly and place your hands on the back of your head," he ordered Laudabaker, determined to get the kid secured before he had a chance to make a run for it.

As the punk complied, Dillon motioned for the clerk to back away. Then he grabbed Laudabaker's left wrist and felt the young man tense under his fingers.

"Don't do it, kid. You're already looking at felony charges; don't make it worse."

Laudabaker's posture sagged, and his hands went limp, allowing Dillon to cuff him without resistance. Then, he patted the young man down and found a nine-millimeter pistol in his jacket pocket; the safety wasn't on.

He shook his head. *Idiot.* Laudabaker was lucky he hadn't accidentally shot himself.

Pocketing the handgun, Dillon read the kid his rights. As he finished, he heard sirens in the distance. The cavalry was almost there.

Grabbing the punk by the arm, he pushed him toward the entrance. "Run, and I'll be forced to shoot."

But the warning wasn't necessary. The fight had gone out of Laudabaker. His chin nearly touched his chest as he stared down at his feet.

Dillon was happy to have him compliant, but they'd hardly finished. He was going back in to get the ring, and then they were going to discuss where the rest of the stolen jewelry was.

* * * *

Dillon

Dillon was right; the kid hadn't been the brightest. Laudabaker stole the jewelry without a plan for how to liquidate it. Though admittedly, starting a relationship with the jewelry store clerk to get access to the jewels *had been* clever. But Laudabaker's plan hadn't stretched beyond that.

Clueless and desperate for some quick cash, he'd gone to Bunker's with Lydia's ring to try and pawn it for a few hundred dollars. Now, he'd be spending Christmas in jail, and the best he could hope for was a hot meal because the only gifts Santa would be bringing him were the kind that came with years of confinement.

Dillon patted the ring in the chest pocket of his blue dress shirt. He'd gotten his Christmas gift and hoped Lydia would give him another.

Glancing at her where she sat in the passenger seat beside him, his breath caught. She was a siren with her dark hair waving around her shoulders and those ocean-colored eyes painted so that his attention was inevitably drawn there.

No matter what her answer was, he couldn't lose her. If she needed more time, he'd give it to her.

He turned his eyes back to the road. They were on their way to his brother's house. Everyone was gathering at Whiteford Farm for Christmas Eve dinner and the annual tree trimming.

As they got closer, his heart rate jumped. He was really doing this. He'd started to sweat despite the chill that lingered in the car. He hadn't been this nervous since the seventh grade when he'd asked his first girl to the school dance. How had Jake gotten through it?

Things were going well with Lydia, but she'd rejected him before. He wished she wouldn't do it again on every Christmas star they passed.

What if she thought it was too fast?

Hell, they'd only been together for five months. Well, it'd been only four since she'd agreed to go out with him, but time didn't matter. He knew she was it for him, so why wait any longer?

"Oh!" she exclaimed, pulling him out of the anxious spiral his thoughts had become. "Look how pretty it all is. The lights and the snow! It's like a winter wonderland."

She turned to him with a bright smile on her face, and he relaxed a little as he took in her delight with the Christmas decorations Jake installed every year.

A twinkle-lighted fence lined the drive to the sprawling modern ranch, and the trees on either side were similarly decorated. Everything shone with warm white light, and with the snow, it did look like a winter wonderland.

"Wait 'til you see the house." He winked at her, but then his thoughts spiraled again. The house. Where he was going to propose to her.

Fuck! He should've come up with some elaborate way to pop the question.

He'd heard about guys spelling out "Will you marry me?"

in Christmas lights. She would have loved that.

His expression turned into a frown as he thought about how focused he'd been on getting the ring back when he should have been planning the proposal. He ran a hand through his hair in frustration just as she let a low squeal.

"Wow. You weren't kidding."

The modern ranch home appeared at the end of the drive, shining brighter than any of the lights they'd passed so far. White lights dotted the sprawling roofline and each of the windows. The tallest one boasted a large wreath nearly half its size.

Dillon knew it was handmade with real boughs because Jake replaced it yearly. There would be more inside, making the whole house smell like Christmas with its piney scent.

A lighted garland with elegant burlap bows swagged across the timber-framed portico while lighted fir trees in silver pots framed the large front door. It was similarly decorated with a lighted garland and a fresh wreath.

"Yeah, Jake kind of goes all out for Christmas." He smiled at her, determined to let go of the anxiety and enjoy this time with his family—no matter how the evening turned out.

When he pulled to a stop, she said, "I can't wait to see the inside."

He grinned at her as he put the car in park. "I don't know. I kind of like having you all to myself." Leaning over, he placed soft kisses on her neck. "How about we turn the car around and—"

Lydia giggled as his breath tickled her. Pulling away,

she said, "Absolutely not!" Turning to him with mock sternness on her face, she added, "Lieutenant, we are spending Christmas Eve with your family, and if you don't stop being naughty . . . well, you might not get the present I had planned for you later."

When she raised an eyebrow at him, Dillon groaned. The woman was a temptress. She managed to light a fire in his blood with one look.

Undoing her seatbelt in one quick motion, he pulled her as close to him as he could and captured her mouth. The damned center console got in the way, but he wasn't about to let that stop him.

She opened those soft lips for him, and he drank in her sweet warmth. Her hands moved to his shoulders, and he wasn't sure if she would push him away or pull him closer.

Knowing if they kept at it, he'd need a minute before he could go in, he broke the kiss. Their breathing had quickened; she was as wound up as he was. Her lips were swollen, and her eyes had darkened the way they did whenever she was turned on.

He raised his eyebrow at her this time. "Okay, Doc. You win."

She looked confused, then her expression cleared, and she huffed out a breath before turning away and climbing out of the car.

Chuckling, he followed her in a considerably better mood. He didn't even mind the cold. Grabbing for her hand as he joined her at the front of the car, he placed a soft kiss on it and smiled down at her. "I love you, Lydia."

Her expression softened. "I love you too, Dillon." The

front door opened as she reached up with her free hand to frame his face.

A pair of red spaniels came barreling out, all gangly legs and floppy ears.

"Oh, how cute!" She bent down to pet the puppies as they jumped up on her legs and yipped.

"Rusty! Ruby! Down!"

At the shout, Dillon glanced toward the front door, where a petite blonde had appeared.

"I'm so sorry, you two. Well, I guess you've met the newest members of our family." Blair chuckled as the pups raced back to her side. "These little ones are still in training."

He had to grin at his brother, who'd joined Blair on the porch. "Christmas gift, I take it?" he asked Blair.

"Yes!" She smiled over at her husband. "Though it came a little early."

Dillon and Lydia climbed the steps hand in hand and met Jake and Blair on the porch.

After a round of hellos and hugs, Lydia bent back down and rubbed two pale pink bellies when Blair asked, "Aren't they great?"

"Adorable!" Lydia smiled up at him, and he knew she was getting ideas.

Oh man, no, no, no. Engagement first, a house next, then maybe they'd think about a puppy.

"Hey, how about we take this party inside?"

Jake laughed. "Cold again, Dill?"

He wouldn't give his brother the satisfaction of agreeing with him. He *was* cold, but more importantly, he wanted to distract Lydia.

Blair slapped Jake on the arm. "Of course, he's cold. It's freezing out here." She gestured for them to follow. "Please come inside."

As he passed by his brother, he mumbled, "Couldn't get just one, huh?"

Jake grinned. "I did. One for me and one for her."

* * * *

Lydia

Lydia concentrated on squeezing the white frosting into a straight line down the ridge of the piece of gingerbread house Daisy held steady for her. They'd taken over the large center island that dominated the kitchen, covering it in various parts of gingerbread housing, candy decorations, and colorful frostings.

Dillon's twin sister had the same bright blue eyes and raven hair, which she blew out of her face as Lydia focused on her task. She was in the kitchen with Blair, Daisy, and their mother, Sandy, from whom the Redland twins had inherited those blue eyes.

Lydia felt at home with these women and let their conversation wash over her as she concentrated. Sandy's short, light brown hair brushed her cheeks as she leaned forward to peer into the wall-mounted oven. She stopped talking and started humming while she checked the baking gingerbread men.

Across the room, Blair mixed more cookie batter at the counter and sang along to the Christmas carols playing from the speaker in the ceiling. The entire home had a built-in sound system, and Sandy had demanded festive music as soon as she'd ushered them all into the kitchen.

Lydia wasn't sure where Dillon or the other Redland men had gotten to, but she'd been given a job and was determined to do it well. She'd almost finished the second line when the frosting bag exploded.

"Oh no!" Daisy exclaimed.

She'd shut her eyes instinctively but felt the sticky goo hit her face and hair.

Where the kitchen had been full of feminine voices a moment ago, it was suddenly as quiet as a tomb, well, a tomb with Christmas music piped in.

Lydia dared to open her eyes to take stock of the damage. She glanced down at her red button-up blouse and was relieved to find it unscathed. The candy-cane striped apron Sandy had thrust on her had taken most of the white shrapnel.

Daisy offered her a paper towel with a sheepish smile. "I guess it could have been worse."

Sandy burst out laughing, and it was contagious. Before she knew it, they were all practically in tears. Jake, Dillon, and their father, Brock, walked into the kitchen, followed by the puppies, who, upon hearing the excitement, joined in with yips and yaps of their own.

The men must have heard the raucous and been curious about what was going on. They were a tall, dark, and handsome trio, though Brock's hair had started to gray. The sight of all three of them together typically made Lydia smile.

Now, she was too busy wiping tears from her eyes to notice. As Dillon came to her rescue, she tried to explain in between fits of giggles.

He grabbed a towel off the counter to wipe the frosting off her face, and she struggled to control the laughter shaking her body.

"There's still a little in your hair," he told her with a grin.

She wiped at a tear that had escaped. Still chuckling, she tried to say, "Oh—my—goodness! I think—I'm banned from gingerbread decorating." More laughs escaped, and she hiccupped. "I can't stop."

The other three women were in similar fits, unable to stop laughing.

"Why don't you try the bathroom? I'm sure the frosting will come out of your hair with a little water. If it doesn't, that's okay. You'll smell sweet and sugary." He winked and turned her toward the hall.

Still laughing, Lydia took his advice and went to the guest bathroom to work on her hair before she turned into a sticky mess.

* * * *

Lydia

A couple of hours later, after Lydia had gotten most of the gingerbread frosting out of her hair, they were all gathered around the twelve-foot tree that dominated the corner of Jake and Blair's living room. It was a live tree and the largest she'd seen in a home before, but it was the perfect fit for the high ceiling.

They'd spent the last half hour decorating it. Everyone had carved out their corner, and the process hadn't taken long with seven people working on it. Now, it was time to light it.

Blair stood on the stepladder with the last decoration for the tree in her hand. It was a large angel with a flowing gold dress, holding a candle in her clasped hands that would light up when plugged in.

Jake had already connected the plug to the other light strings, and Lydia heard Blair let out a little cry in triumph as she stretched on her toes and just managed to place the topper on the tree.

"Wonderful!" Sandy clasped her hands together, her eyes glowing at the beautiful sight. Brock wrapped his arm around her shoulder as they stared at the shiny topper.

"Come on, Jake. I want to see it with lights," Daisy complained.

Jake helped Blair down and moved the stepladder out of the way. Holding the switch, he waited for everyone's attention to return to the tree before pushing it on.

There were a lot of "oohs" and "ahhs" as they all took in the glistening tree. It *was* rather impressive. All twelve feet of the Christmas tree were covered in twinkling lights, white and gold ornaments, and now the beautiful golden angel.

Lydia felt Dillon's arm come around her, and she leaned into his side as they stared at the beautiful sight. "This is a nice tradition."

"It is. We've always trimmed the tree together on Christmas Eve. I'm glad you could be a part of it this year."

He kissed the top of her head and made her smile.

She couldn't remember the last time she'd had so much fun at Christmas. Not since her mom had passed, anyway. Christmas in Greece with her father just wasn't the same. Not when it was sunny, and there was no snow.

She was glad she'd decided to stay in Rolling Brook for this year's holiday. Baba understood, and he'd get a nice surprise in a few months.

Thinking about her gift for Dillon, she couldn't contain the excitement that bubbled up. "Presents!"

Moving out of his embrace, she went searching for the small package she'd placed under the tree when they'd first arrived.

Everyone sprang into action around her as they grabbed their gifts. Finding the small rectangular box she'd wrapped for Dillon, she brought it to where he reclined on the oversized leather couch. He'd been the only one not racing for the tree at her announcement.

Curious about that, she handed him the package with hands that trembled in excitement and maybe a little bit of nerves.

I hope he likes it!

"Merry Christmas, Dillon." She smiled, but butterflies fluttered in her stomach.

He accepted the package with a grin and tore into it. The silver ribbon and green paper were quickly discarded to reveal a thin white box. She held her breath as he opened it.

When he pulled out the plane tickets, he looked up at her.

"Surprise!" She chewed on her lower lip while she waited for his response.

He looked a little dazed. "This is what you've been hiding from me? A trip to Greece?"

"Yes! I was so worried you would find out and ruin the surprise. Do you like it?"

When he continued to simply stare at her, she added, "We don't have to go if you don't want to."

He seemed to shake himself and stood abruptly. "My turn."

"What?" She frowned in confusion, but he grabbed her hand and led her to the doorway, where a ball of mistletoe hung.

"Lydia, you're the only Christmas present I need, and I would love to go to Greece with you."

She smiled in relief, but he wasn't finished. Dillon dropped to one knee, and her free hand flew to her mouth. "Oh!"

He pulled a ring out of his pocket and held it up to her. "Lydia Elena Pallas Mason, will you give me the best Christmas gift I could ask for and agree to be my wife?"

Her legs felt weak, and she fell to her knees in front of him. As her heart raced, warmth radiated throughout her body. "Yes! Of course, I will."

She reached for him and placed quick, excited kisses all over his face. Under her palms, she felt his cheeks lift into a smile. Pulling back, she took in this amazing man who was going to be her husband. She'd been so sure she was rushing things that she couldn't believe this was happening.

"Am I dreaming?"

"Not unless I am, too," he told her with a smile. "Here, let's make sure it fits. This ring went through a lot to be here today."

"What do you mean?" she asked as he slid the ring on her finger.

He chuckled. "I'll tell you about it . . . later."

The ring was a perfect fit. She held up her left hand, admiring it. "It's beautiful, Dillon. I love it!"

Raising her eyes from her new favorite accessory, she caught him grinning at her. "You owe me one more gift, Doc."

She raised a brow. "I do?"

He stood and helped her to her feet, then pointed up. She followed his finger to the ball of mistletoe hanging above their heads.

Chuckling, she leaned into him. "I think I can handle that, Lieutenant."

As their lips touched, she heard cheers, clapping, and barking in the background.

Pulling back with a grin, she murmured, "We have an audience."

He still held her in his arms, and she didn't ever want to leave them. "They probably want to congratulate me on my new fiancé."

"We should probably let them." She couldn't stop smiling as they turned to Dillon's family—her family.

With linked hands, they joined the group, eagerly waiting to see the ring and offer their best wishes. Christmas had just become her favorite holiday, and this one was undoubtedly the best yet.

A NOTE TO READERS

If you enjoyed this book, please consider leaving a review. They help spread the word about my books through the recommendation process and help new readers decide if they'll be a good fit for them. Reviews also contribute to my rankings on sites like Amazon, making my stories more visible to new readers. Even a one-line review makes a difference!

If you can't get enough of Rolling Brook or the Redlands, pick up *Small Town Frame-up* to read Daisy's story! She's in trouble, and the one man who can get her out of it is the same one who's been trying to avoid her. Can she convince Jameson to let go of his idea of her as "off limits," or will forces beyond their control rob them of the chance?

If you'd like a free novella set in the Rolling Brook world, subscribe to my newsletter. By signing up, you receive an EXCLUSIVE book featuring a woman on the run and forced proximity with a troubled military hero.

Want more updates, teasers, and giveaways? Follow me on social media.

All my links can be found here: https://linktr.ee/blyedonovan.

Thank you for reading!

xoxo,

Blye Donovan

ACKNOWLEDGMENTS

While I love a "happy for now" ending, Dillon demanded a "happy ever after." Of course, Lydia wasn't going to make that easy on him. He had just enough of the grump left in him to play the Grinch in their bonus epilogue. I think both their hearts grew a few sizes by the end of it. I know mine did.

I have to thank my wonderful husband for taking me to the Biltmore Estate in order to get me in the holiday mood to write their love story.

My family and friends—Heather and Cheryl—thank you for reading through my rough drafts and providing feedback. Writing may happen in a vacuum, but it's others reading that writing that truly matters.

My critique partner, Nina F. Thank you for your invaluable input. I am very grateful for the time you gave me as I know you don't have much to spare.

Lastly, thank you to all the readers who cheered on Dillon and Lydia. Your support means more than I could ever hope to express.

BOOKS BY BLYE DONOVAN

Rolling Brook Protectors
Hunted at Whiteford Farm
Gifts from a Stalker
Small Town Frame-up
Condemned by Secrets
Marked as Queen of Hearts

Stand-alone Novels
Undercover Santa
Blaze of Glory

Texas Heat Shared Series
Wait for You

TOP Security Series
Going Rogue

ABOUT THE AUTHOR

Blye Donovan is a military brat and a veteran who resides in the Lowcountry of South Carolina with her husband and fur-child, Maximus. Besides books, she's addicted to coffee, peanut butter, and shoes. When she's not feeding these addictions, she writes books  that are romantic suspense stories featuring strong heroines and alpha protector heroes overcoming dangerous villains. Her books are often set in small towns because she loves the atmosphere associated with them, especially when they have historic architecture. She was supposed to become a historic preservationist, but . . . writing has always been her passion. You can check out her current series, follow her on social media, and more all at this link: https://linktr.ee/blyedonovan.